Over the loudspeaker they were announcing the final heat.

"Guess I better get going," Kennin said, and got into the Corolla.

Angelita reached into the car and patted him on the helmet. "Have fun."

He lined up next to Chris in *Slide or Die*. The two drivers nodded at each other.

Derek stepped between the cars and bent down so he could speak to both drivers at the same time. "Glad you two could make it," he said, obviously pleased that Kennin and Chris were running against each other in the final heat. "Now remember. It's not just about winning. It's about the show."

sidewayz glory

By Todd Strasser

ILLUSTRATED BY CRAIG PHILLIPS

Simon Pulse
New York   London   Toronto   Sydney

〰

SIMON PULSE

An imprint of Simon & Schuster Children's Publishing Division

1230 Avenue of the Americas, New York, NY 10020

Text copyright © 2006 by Todd Strasser

Illustrations copyright © 2006 by Craig Phillips

All rights reserved, including the right of reproduction in whole or in part in any form.

SIMON PULSE and colophon are registered trademarks of Simon & Schuster, Inc.

Designed by Sammy Yuen Jr.

The text of this book was set in Trade Gothic.

Manufactured in the United States of America

First Simon Pulse edition July 2006

10 9 8 7 6 5 4 3 2 1

Library of Congress Control Number 2005930632

ISBN-13: 978-1-4169-0583-7

ISBN-10: 1-4169-0583-9

This book is dedicated to
Lia "Check Out That Jag" Strasser

I would like to thank the following organization and people for their mostly helpful (and sometimes humorously wiseass) comments and assistance:

Amanda Sohr, Dan Carluch, DGTrials.com, Troy "Driftmonkey" Holloway, Chachi, Alex, Thoraxe, LookOutMatt, Gram, I Love Sweatpants, d4vech3n, EunosGangstarr, Darkbane, 1.8turbo510, Shiftnslide, Die Screaming, Airjockie, Dr. Baby, Drift Machine, Thon, Dragracingunderground, VQ Driver, ECDA, Knives, Kata, Toycoma, Mikespeed95, fraggleSTICKcar, Ichi-Go, Dominican Drift, Drew, Davis, Mistatwo, Thrwnsprkz, Moorefire, Saru of the West, Forsaken TH, Trunk, Dave Chen, Dori FC, Vosko, Mranlet.

sidewayz glory

1

Kennin's memory was a blur of broken images and sensations going back to the start of the battle drift. The moment the 240 SX broke traction, he'd felt a shimmy in the steering. He should have quit the tsuiso then, but he didn't. Going into the first turn, he'd felt a heavy vibration. Then something let go. The right front dropped and the car slid sideways and began to spin. Yellow and orange sparks flying everywhere, the car swinging wildly around, he'd veered off the road. Rocks, brush, and dust flew in the air and pelted the windshield.

And then . . . *Crash!*

He'd been pinned inside the 240 SX. He remembered the hiss of escaping coolant and the smell of leaking gasoline. But most of the other memories and sensations from that night had been muted, if not entirely washed away, under a wave of searing, throbbing agony from his leg. There'd been the high-pitched whine of the fire department's saw cutting the car open. Red and white lights flashing chaotically in the dark. Hands reaching in, grabbing his clothes, and tugging him out of the wrecked vehicle; every movement a blast of unbearable red-hot pain. More hands lifting and laying him on a gurney. Faces staring down at him, lips moving, jumbled words and questions. The scream that tore through his throat, born of intolerable pain, when they'd placed the temporary inflatable cast around his left leg and then strapped him down. He hadn't even felt the injection, just the welcome relief as the painkiller went to work.

Then the bright lights inside the ambulance. A female EMS tech with brown hair squeezing his hand and saying he was going to be okay. Next they pulled the gurney out of the ambulance and rolled him through the cool air into the hospital. Long fluorescent lights in the ceiling of the hospital emergency room. More faces hovering over him, lips moving, hazy jumbles of words. The antiseptic smell of alcohol. Big gray sheets of X-ray film being passed around. Rolling down a corridor and into a cold room with lots of polished stainless steel. A clear plastic mask over his nose and mouth. Someone told him to count to ten.

He opened his eyes. He was in a hospital bed with metal rails, his left leg suspended in the air by a pulley hanging from a rack overhead. Tubes ended in needles stuck into the crook of his arm and the back of his hand. Dull throbbing pain rose from his left leg. His sister, Shinchou, was sitting in a chair against the wall reading *People* magazine. He closed his eyes.

When he next opened them, the room was dark. A machine close by was beeping, and he could hear the sound of steady breathing. Someone was asleep in the bed next to him. His leg hurt, his throat was dry, and he was incredibly thirsty. A plastic cup with a straw sat on the night table beside his bed and he tried to reach for it, but the tubes attached to his arm stopped him.

A male nurse named Leon helped him sip orange juice through a straw. Leon wore a blue hospital shirt and pants. He had dark skin, mischievous eyes, and huge hands. He gave Kennin a button to push whenever the pain got too great. Leon said, "This is your joystick, baby."

Kennin used the joystick sparingly. He'd feel the pain from his leg creeping up, but he'd wait, daring the agony to make him give in. At first it was no contest. The pain roared down on him like an avalanche and there was no fighting back. He'd pump the joystick and grimace until the drugs brought relief.

Leon came back. "How's it hangin', dawg?"

"Okay, I guess," Kennin answered, lifting the joystick slightly. "As long as I have this."

"Oh, yeah, push that button and life is easy." Leon grinned.

"What's the story with my leg?" Kennin asked.

Leon's eyebrows went up. "They didn't tell you? Lemme see." He picked up a chart hanging at the base of the hospital bed and thumbed through the pages. "Busted up pretty good, my friend. Broke in two places. You got a few screws here and there, but not enough to open a hardware store."

"How much longer am I in here for?" Kennin asked.

"Short as possible," Leon said, flipping to another page on the chart. "You're our least favorite kind of patient."

"What kind's that?" Kennin asked.

"The nonpaying kind. No money, no health insurance, no nothin'." Leon closed the chart. "What'd you do, crawl out of a hole somewhere? Who takes care of you, dawg? I mean, when you're not in here."

"I take care of myself," Kennin said.

"Oh yeah?" Leon looked at Kennin's leg, suspended in the air. "Don't look like you're doing a real good job, bro."

Kennin shrugged. "So, I didn't get an answer to my question. How long am I here?"

"Hey, I ain't no doctor, but based on what I've seen, they gotta wait for the surgical wounds to start to heal. Soon as the wounds look like they're healing okay, they'll probably wrap that leg in plaster and kick your sorry butt into the street. Free up this bed for some paying customer."

"But that'll be what? A few days? A week?" Kennin asked.

"I'd guess a week or less," said Leon. "Why? What's the rush?"

Kennin wanted to know what had happened to the car. Why it had gone out of control right at the start of the tsu-iso. It wasn't like he'd done anything to cause the crash. He'd hardly gotten going. And why, just before the start, had he heard that impact wrench?

The answer he gave Leon was, "Who wants to be in a hospital?"

"That's the spirit, dawg." Leon grinned. "Get out of this bed and let us make some money off someone who can pay."

Leon left. Kennin settled back in the bed and clicked through the TV channels. Here in the hospital he had close to twenty. Sure beat the five they had in the trailer.

Shinchou came back. She had dark rings under her eyes, and her long black hair, usually so well kept, looked stringy and unwashed. She was thinner, too. Her clothes—stained and dirty—hung off her as if she were a human clothes hanger. Her skin was so pale it almost appeared translucent.

"How are you?" she asked.

"Okay," Kennin said. "How about you?"

She shrugged and pulled her yellowed, nicotine-stained fingers through her dark hair.

"What's going on?" Kennin asked.

Shinchou shrugged.

"You don't look well," Kennin said.

His sister shook her head as if to indicate that she didn't want to talk about it. Maybe it wasn't necessary. It was pretty easy to guess what was going on.

"Still dancing?" Kennin asked.

Shinchou nodded. She crossed one leg over the other and swung it rapidly. At the same time her hands kept moving, tugging at her hair and scratching her arms. It seemed as if she couldn't keep still.

"How much do you still owe Jack?" Kennin asked.

She rolled her eyes as if to say it was none of his business. He knew that asking more questions would just make her mad, so instead they watched an episode of *The Simpsons* on the hospital room TV. When it was over, Shinchou stood up.

"I'm gonna go have a smoke," she said, and went out.

She didn't come back.

2

Something smelled sweet. Kennin thought he was dreaming, but when he opened his eyes, Mariel Lewis was standing beside his bed, looking down at him. She was wearing a tight pink sweater that spoke volumes about what was underneath. Her blond hair was hooked behind her ears and her lips glistened with lip gloss.

"I tried not to wake you," she said.

"You didn't." Kennin yawned and started to stretch his arms, but the tubes stopped him. "I think your perfume did."

"How are you feeling?" Her gold earrings glimmered.

"Okay, I guess," Kennin answered.

"Everyone thought you were dead," she said.

"Huh?"

"I mean, that night. The way the side of the car was crushed in."

Kennin blinked. It was strange, but until now, no one

had spoken of what actually happened. "How long ago was it?"

"The crash?" Mariel gazed up at the ceiling and counted on her fingers. "Five days?"

It felt like a month to Kennin. "Looked pretty bad, huh?"

"You can't imagine," Mariel said. She had a way of licking her lips when she spoke. And her blue eyes never left his. "They say you were lucky. I'm glad you're still alive."

"That makes two of us," said Kennin.

"When do you think you'll get out of here?"

"They tell me another week maybe."

"I'm looking forward to seeing you." She reached over and stroked his cheek with her fingers. "I mean, once you get out of this place."

Tito and Angelita walked in. They were both wearing hoodies. Tito's was gray and the hood covered his head. Angelita's was navy blue with the hood down, her black hair pulled back into a ponytail. When she saw Mariel leaning over Kennin in the bed, she froze.

"Oops. Sorry, dude, didn't mean to butt in," Tito said. He and Angelita started to back out of the room.

Mariel straightened up. Her eyes met Angelita's and a smile appeared on her lips. "It's okay, I was just leaving."

Tito hesitated. "You sure?"

"Yes," Mariel said, then leaned over to kiss Kennin. He turned his head slightly so it was only half on the lips.

"Can't wait to see you again," she whispered, just loudly enough for Tito and Angelita to hear. "In private."

Mariel picked up a white jacket from the chair beside the bed and then started out of the room. But as she passed Angelita, she paused. "Sorry about your car."

Angelita started to nod, mistakenly assuming the words were sincere.

But Mariel wasn't finished. "Guess you'll have to find some other way to keep the boys interested."

Angelita flushed. Mariel stopped in the doorway, turned to Kennin, and fluttered her fingers. "Bye."

The blonde left. Angelita had to restrain herself from whaling on her. She took a deep breath and stared at the TV, unable to look Kennin in the eye.

"What was *that* about?" Tito asked.

"Not what it looked like," Kennin said, his eyes on Angelita.

"If that wasn't what it looked like, then what was it?" Tito asked. Now Angelita gazed at Kennin. Her brother had asked exactly what she was wondering.

"I don't know," Kennin said. "I'm stuck in this bed and can't move. Anyone who comes in here can do pretty much what they want to me."

"Chris Craven sees her doing that with you and he'll be the next one in here . . . with a baseball bat," Tito said. "You'll wind up in a full-body cast with less teeth than my grandmother."

"Thanks, I'll keep it in mind," Kennin said, and turned to Angelita. "How's the car?"

Angelita looked down at the floor. "Totaled."

Kennin winced. That was terrible news. He felt both awful and responsible. "Insurance?"

Tito's sister shook her head. "Denied. The accident report has the driver wearing a racing helmet, and the police say it had all the markings of a street race. I didn't even bother with a claim. They'd disallow it in a second."

"I'm really sorry," Kennin said miserably. "You were counting on selling that car to make money for college."

"I salvaged the engine and some of the mods," Angelita said. "That's where most of the money was. There are still plenty of 240 SXs around. I'll find one."

Kennin turned to Tito. "So what happened with the tsuiso?"

"We lost big-time," Tito answered. "You almost lost your leg. My sister lost her car. And I lost all my cash."

"I'm sorry about that," Kennin said, although he'd never wanted Tito to bet on him in the first place.

"Not as sorry as I am, dude," Tito said. "But what can you do? Accidents happen, you know?"

Accidents? Kennin thought uncertainly, recalling the sound of the impact wrench and the way the car had started to vibrate the moment the tsuiso began. "Did anyone ever figure out what happened?"

Tito glanced at his sister and then said, "The wheel

broke off. Right where the spokes meet the center cap. Crappy aftermarket knockoffs."

"They weren't knockoffs," Angelita shot back in a way that made Kennin suspect they'd had this argument before.

"Someone could have pawned them off on you without you knowing it," Tito said.

"I'd know," Angelita retorted.

An awkward silence followed.

"If it wasn't the wheels, then what else could it have been?" Kennin finally asked.

"I don't know," Angelita said. "Nothing makes sense. The car ran perfectly the heat before. If there'd been anything wrong, you would have felt it during the drive back up the mountain."

"Unless it was a cheap wheel and it just broke," Tito said.

Angelita's face hardened with anger and she glared at her brother. "For the last time: It was *not* a cheap wheel."

They'd reached a stalemate. Angelita's tone implied that there'd be no more discussion on the topic. Tito looked at Kennin. "You made the newspapers again. There's been this big public outcry. Street racing is dangerous to law-abiding citizens. It has to be stopped. Innocent people are going to be injured. Blah, blah, blah . . ."

"They didn't mention me by name, did they?" Kennin asked.

Tito shook his head. "No, 'cause you're still a minor."

"So when do you get out?" Angelita asked.

"About a week, I think," said Kennin. "But it'll be a while before the cast comes off."

An awkward silence followed. Finally Tito said, "Hey, Angie, think I could have a private moment with *mi amigo*?"

Angelita frowned, but then nodded and stepped out into the hall. Tito moved closer to Kennin and said in a low voice, "Two months from now, she's out of here."

Kennin scowled. "What do you mean?"

"I mean, she's got enough credits to graduate from Dorado by Christmas," Tito explained. "Then she moves to California, establishes residence, and pays in-state tuition next year. There's only one thing that can stop her, dude, and that's you."

Tito paused and gave Kennin a meaningful look. "She's still hung up on you. She won't admit it, but I can see it in her eyes. You gotta do the right thing, man. You gotta let her go, okay?"

Kennin didn't answer. It still rankled him that Tito didn't think he was good enough for Angelita. But Tito was right about one thing: Angelita had worked really hard to get good grades and save money so she could go to college in California. And Kennin didn't want to stand in the way.

Tito pressed on. "It's no big deal, right? You can get any babe you want. I saw what was going down with Mariel when we got here. She's the hottest chick around, and all you gotta do is snap your fingers."

Kennin nodded slowly. *Maybe . . . Maybe not.*

Leon came in and took the joystick away. "Fun's over, dawg. No more of this for you."

"How come?" Kennin asked.

"They don't want you to get used to it," Leon said as he removed the IV from the back of Kennin's hand. "This is a hospital, not an introduction to Junkie 101. Believe me, I've been there. I know."

"You were a junkie?" Kennin asked.

"Let's just say that for a time I followed the path of the unenlightened," Leon said, and unhooked the small clear plastic bag from the IV stand.

"How'd you get off it?" Kennin asked, thinking of Shinchou.

"Sista Bertha. She runs a rehab clinic over on the south side. Place looks like a dump, but believe me, she knows what she's doing."

"What's it cost?" Kennin asked.

"It don't cost nothin', dawg," Leon said. "Sista's doin' God's work. She gives you one shot at redemption, understand? The second time you fall from grace, you fall alone."

"I'll keep it in mind," Kennin said.

"So, how come you never told me you were some kind of outlaw celebrity race car driver?" Leon asked.

"You sure you got the right guy?" Kennin asked.

"You didn't bust up that leg playin' soccer, right?" Leon said, then leaned close and lowered his voice. "There's a cop outside waitin' to talk to you. Want me to tell him you're not up to it?"

Kennin thought it over. "Thanks, but I can deal."

Leon went to the door and stuck his head out into the hall. A moment later Detective Sam Neilson of the Las Vegas Police came in. Neilson had blond hair and was wearing a tan sports jacket and dark slacks. He'd lost weight since the last time Kennin had seen him.

"How's the leg?" Neilson asked.

"Getting better," Kennin replied. "I like the look."

Neilson smiled, as if pleased that someone had noticed. "Yeah, I dropped twenty pounds and got some new threads." He touched his upper lip. "You like it better without the mustache?"

Kennin tried to remember what the detective looked like with the mustache. "Yeah, I think so."

"Okay." Neilson grinned, as if he was pleased he'd made the right decision. Then, like everyone else who visited, he asked how much longer Kennin would be in the hospital. Kennin told him a week.

"Then what?" the detective asked.

"Sorry?" Kennin didn't follow.

"No more street racing," Neilson said.

Kennin remained silent.

"It's bad enough that we gotta deal with DWIs and all that crap without a bunch of kids whipping sideways around corners at a hundred miles an hour," Neilson said.

"Not quite that fast," Kennin said.

"Whatever. You know how many violations we could've hit you with?" Neilson asked. "Driving without a license, reckless endangerment, speeding . . . believe me, it was quite a list."

"How come you didn't?" Kennin asked.

Neilson drummed his fingers against the bed's chrome rail. "Turns out you've got friends in high places."

Kennin frowned.

"Come on, Kennin," Neilson said. "Think about it. Can't be like you've got *that* many friends in *that* many high places, can it?"

Mercado, Kennin realized. The owner of the Babylon Casino. *But why?*

"You've been the subject of several conversations down at headquarters," Neilson went on. "There was even some talk about handing you over to social services."

"You can't do that," Kennin said. "My sister's my legal guardian."

"Where've you been, kid? Your sister's a stripper on crystal meth. She's no help to you or herself."

Kennin winced. So there it was—confirmation of his worst fears. Anger welled up inside him. He knew his sister well enough to know she hadn't gotten there alone. She'd had help.

Neilson slid his hand along the chrome rail. "And there's still the matter of the stolen GTO. Mark my words, Kennin, sooner or later that one's gonna come back to haunt you."

"Seriously, Detective Neilson?" Kennin said. "I've never stolen a car in my life."

"Oh yeah?" Neilson said. "Swear on your mother's grave that you had absolutely nothing to do with that car."

Kennin turned and gazed out the window at the purplish gray mountains in the distance. Neilson nodded, as if he'd expected just such a response. "This is my last warning, Kennin. When you get out of this bed, stay out of cars and off the street. 'Cause next time no one's gonna be able to save you."

3

The doctor said he could leave the hospital, but the rules stated that Kennin couldn't just limp out on crutches. Someone had to come get him. He spoke to Shinchou on the phone, and she said she'd pick him up at noon.

Noon came and went and Shinchou didn't show.

The afternoon dragged on. Kennin tried to call a few more times, but she didn't answer.

At six p.m. Leon stuck his head into the room. "Ride didn't come?"

Kennin didn't reply. The answer was obvious.

Leon let out a low sigh. "Give me ten, dawg. I'll be back."

Fifteen minutes later Leon returned wearing his street clothes—jeans and a gray UNLV sweatshirt—and pushing a wheelchair. "You ready?" he asked, then grinned. "Just kidding. I know you been ready since noon."

Leon helped him into the wheelchair. Out in the corridor they went through a puke green door marked HOSPITAL PERSONNEL ONLY, and then through another door. A pair of metal crutches was leaning against the wall. Leon looked around to make sure no one was watching, then picked up the crutches and put them in Kennin's lap. "Here's a going-away present."

Kennin held the crutches in his lap, and Leon pushed the wheelchair through another door to the outside and past a sign that said EMPLOYEE PARKING LOT. For the first time in nearly two weeks, Kennin breathed fresh air. It was mid-November and, at six thirty in the evening, already dark. Kennin felt a chill and shivered.

"Yeah, it's gotten a little cooler these last few weeks," said Leon. "Down into the low fifties at night." He stopped the wheelchair next to a bright red Chevy Silverado with big chrome rims and tinted windows.

"Nice ride," Kennin said.

"The poor man's Escalade," Leon quipped, opening the passenger-side door for Kennin and helping him in. Kennin's blue fiberglass cast went from his hip to his ankle, and moving around wasn't easy. Once he was comfortable, Leon got into the driver's seat. "Where to, Captain?"

"North Las Vegas," Kennin said. "Trailer park called the Sierra Ne-Vue."

"Oh yeah," Leon said as they pulled out of the hospital

parking lot. "The high-rent district." This too was a joke. If Las Vegas had a slum, the Sierra Ne-Vue was probably it.

Twenty minutes later they passed the dead brown palm trees at the entrance to the trailer park.

"That one," Kennin said, pointing at the trailer with a bright yellow 'vette parked outside it.

"Whoa, nice ride," Leon said when he saw the 'vette. "That yours?"

"No," Kennin replied.

"Sorry to hear it," Leon said.

Not as sorry as I am to see that car, Kennin thought.

They pulled up next to the 'vette. Leon was helping Kennin out when the door to the trailer opened and Jack the jackass and Shinchou came out. As usual, Jack was wearing a black cowboy hat, a black shirt, and lots of gold jewelry. Even though it was getting dark, Shinchou was wearing a pair of sunglasses. But Kennin could see that the left side of her face was swollen and bruised.

"What happened?" Kennin asked, leaning on the crutches.

Shinchou's hand immediately went to her face. "Nothing. I banged myself."

Kennin didn't believe her. "I meant at the hospital. You were supposed to pick me up."

"Oh, sorry." His sister hung her head. "I forgot."

"How's the leg?" Jack asked.

"What do you care?" Kennin asked back.

Jack's face hardened. "You ought to show more respect, pardner."

"I show respect to people who deserve it," Kennin replied.

Jack slid his hand through Shinchou's arm and led her toward the 'vette. Kennin's sister was unsteady on her feet and almost stumbled.

"So what did happen to your face?" Kennin asked.

"I told you, I bumped it," she said.

"How?"

"Butt out," Jack growled as he opened the 'vette's door for Shinchou.

Kennin ignored him. "Where're you going?" he asked his sister.

"To work," Shinchou said.

"With your eye like that?"

"I said, butt out," Jack snarled, placing his hand on Shinchou's shoulder and guiding her into the 'vette's passenger seat. Then he came around to the driver's side, where Kennin and Leon were. Jack started to open the door, but Kennin lifted a crutch and blocked him.

Jack glared at Kennin. "Move it."

Kennin kept the crutch where it was. "I don't like what you're doing to my sister."

"She can take care of herself," Jack said.

"How many other girls have you said that about?" Kennin asked. "And how did they wind up?"

"I don't know what you're talking about," Jack said.

"How about the blonde with the hot pink streaks?" Kennin asked.

Jack glanced into the 'vette. Shinchou had leaned her head back against the car seat, her eyes closed as if she was asleep. Seeing that she wasn't paying attention, Jack wheeled around and swung his arm, knocking the crutch out of his way. Kennin instantly lifted the other crutch and held it like a baseball bat, ready to smack Jack's head—complete with cowboy hat—into the upper deck if the guy made a move.

"Whoa!" Leon jumped in between them. "Chill out. Back off."

Jack pointed a finger at Kennin. "You better learn to stay out of other people's business, boy. Ain't you figured that out by now? Ain't you already been hurt bad enough? You don't want to get in another accident, boy. So stay out of my business."

The words struck Kennin as hard as a closed fist. "What are you saying? That what happened wasn't an accident?"

"I'm just sayin', you don't want to get hurt again, stay out of people's business and do what you're told." Jack got into the 'vette and screeched out of the trailer park, leaving a cloud of tire smoke and exhaust.

"Friend of the family?" Leon asked, picking up the crutch Jack had batted away.

"My sister's boyfriend," Kennin replied.

"Looked old enough to be her father."

"Tell me about it," said Kennin.

"A badass?"

"He'd like you to think so."

"Let me help you get inside," Leon said.

"Thanks," said Kennin.

Leon got the door, and Kennin climbed up the loose concrete cinder blocks and went inside. The trailer was filthy. Not just messy, but dirty. It may not have been much of a home, but he and Shinchou had always tried to keep it neat and clean. Now there was garbage scattered around and the place reeked of cigarettes and decaying refuse. Empty food containers, glasses with cigarette butts floating in them, plates with the crusted remains of dinners still sticking to them, empty cans and bottles.

Leon looked around. "Aw, crap," he muttered, "and I thought I was gonna get home on time tonight."

"You still can," Kennin said.

"Right. You gonna clean up this mess all by yourself." Leon rolled up the sleeves of his sweatshirt. "Good thing this place is so small. We should be able to get it fixed up pretty fast."

Normally, Kennin would have refused the offer. He could clean up his own messes, and his sister's. But it would be a difficult job with the cast on.

"Got any garbage bags?" Leon asked.

"Under the sink," Kennin said.

Leon was right. With the two of them working, the cleanup went pretty fast. Kennin stationed himself at the kitchen sink and washed dishes, while Leon did most of the picking up. Before long the trailer almost looked inhabitable again.

"There you go, dawg," Leon said, tying off a big black garbage bag. "Least you can sleep here tonight."

"I don't know how to thank you," Kennin said.

"Hey, no problem," Leon said. "I know you'd do the same for me. There's just one thing." He placed a small glassine envelope and a bloodstained cotton ball on the kitchen counter. "I don't have to tell you what this means, right?"

Kennin felt a deep ache inside. Here was the undeniable proof that Shinchou was doing serious drugs. Just as Neilson had said.

"Sorry to give you the bad news," Leon said. "But I thought you'd want to know."

Kennin nodded slowly, feeling the weight of this new problem press down onto his shoulders.

Leon pulled out a pen and wrote something down. "Here's my phone number and Sista Bertha's address. You want me to help, just let me know."

"Thanks." Kennin took the slip of paper.

"You're wondering what's in this for me, right?" Leon asked with a smile.

Kennin nodded.

"I was once your age and on my own too," Leon said. "So I know how messed up that can be. If it wasn't for a couple of folks who took pity and helped me out, I wouldn't be here today. So I'm just tryin' to do the same for you."

"I appreciate it," Kennin said. "I really do. And thanks again for helping me clean up."

"No prob." Leon picked up the garbage bag. "I'll just take this with me. Good luck, dawg."

Leon left. Kennin stared down at the glassine envelope and the bloody cotton ball. Jack had an ironclad grip on his sister now. As if the five-grand loan and weekly vig wasn't enough, now the bastard had her on crystal meth. Kennin could feel the anger rising in him again. And what about the crash? Jack made it sound like it wasn't an accident. Normally, Kennin thought Jack was full of crap, but not this time. The night of the drift battle Jack had told him to tank the second heat. When Kennin won it instead, the guy was furious and warned him not to even think about winning the last heat. But Jack had no reason to think Kennin would listen. So he could have done something to make sure Kennin wouldn't win. Especially if there was serious money on the line.

In the hallway at Dorado High the next day, Kennin leaned on his crutches and watched Tito in the crowd of guys moving to their next classes. Tito's head was turned toward Mutt, and he was talking excitedly. "The tsuiso thing is over, dude. After what happened to Kennin the cops are doing a full-court press. And it doesn't matter anyway, because the Babylon's opening a drift track. The future's gonna be tandem drifting. Two guys on a course, running full-on side by side, showing the judges what they can do."

Mutt winced slightly. "I don't know about side by side. Sounds like a recipe for some serious bang-ups."

"Sure, if *amateurs* drive," Tito said. "But we're talking professionals. Guys who really know how to drift. That's the whole idea of a team. It's why the Babylon's building a track. Dude, just imagine it. Unlimited seat time. Hours and hours to practice drifting without the cops and crowds and kooks."

"Sounds great," Kennin said.

Tito looked up with a shocked expression. "Wha'?"

"You look like you've just seen a ghost," Kennin said.

"I—I—," Tito stammered. "I just didn't expect to see *you*. When'd you get out?"

"Yesterday," Kennin said.

"How's the leg?" Mutt asked.

"Still attached," said Kennin.

"That's no joke, dude," Mutt said. "I mean, if you'd seen the wreck. Everyone thought you were toast."

"So I hear," said Kennin.

The bell rang, and the bodies in the hallway picked up speed toward their next classes.

"Gotta book," Tito said a little too quickly. Something shimmered in the guy's earlobe. Kennin realized it was a diamond stud.

"Wait," Kennin said.

Tito stopped and bit his lip. "What?"

"See you at lunch?" Kennin asked.

"Uh, yeah, sure, you bet," Tito said, and hurried away.

"He's in school," Angelita's friend Marta whispered in AP Spanish Lit.

Angelita didn't have to ask which "he" she was referring to.

"I saw him in the hall," Marta whispered.

Angelita shrugged.

"Don't give me that act," Marta scoffed. "You *know* you want to see him."

"Shut up," Angelita hissed.

In the front of the room their teacher frowned at them. After all, this was AP Spanish Lit, the most advanced foreign language course at Dorado High, and misbehavior was almost unheard of. Angelita went back to her reading of *La Casa de Bernarda Alba*, a play that explored themes of repression, passion, and conformity while examining the effects of men on women.

Angelita wished Kennin hadn't had such an effect on her. Maybe from the play she would learn something helpful.

Marta was quiet until the class ended. But as soon as the bell rang, she turned once again to Angelita. "Going to lunch?"

"No, why would I?" Angelita replied, although she already knew why her friend had asked.

"Don't play dumb with me," Marta said. She had reddish brown frizzy hair and was short on height but long on sass. Even though Angelita had little to say to her about Kennin, Marta was smart enough to read the signs.

"Okay, you're right," Angelita admitted. "But what's the point?"

"You know you want to see him," Marta said.

"And like I just said, what's the point?" Angelita repeated.

"You got two months left of high school, girl," Marta

said. "Maybe it's time to let yourself have a little fun."

True, Angelita thought. *Why not have a little fun?* But not with Kennin. He wasn't a boy you had "fun" with and then left and forgot about.

"I'll think about it," Angelita said.

"Liar," Marta shot back with a grin.

They parted at the classroom door. Marta headed for the cafeteria and Angelita for auto tech. A quiet lunch with camshafts and fuel injectors was preferable to the noisy cafeteria filled with rude girls and troublemakers. She took her time walking. Soon the hall started to empty. And there he was, at his locker, propped up on his crutches, his black hair falling into his eyes, a green backpack hanging off one shoulder. Angelita instantly felt a familiar nervousness spread over her. It was so strange. She could have walked down this hall a dozen times wishing he'd be there, and he wouldn't be. But this was the one time she wasn't looking for him, and there he was.

Kennin wasn't exactly amped about being back in school. With his leg in a cast and his arms handling crutches, the only way to carry books was in a backpack, and he wasn't used to it. The pack fell to the floor with a thud, and the sound of his annoyed muttering echoed softly down the empty hall as he tried to bend down and pick it up, the long blue cast clearly getting in the way.

"Wait," Angelita called.

He straightened up and looked surprised to see her.

"Don't they usually give you an escort?" she said as she picked up the backpack.

"I didn't want one," he said, taking the backpack from her.

"That's so like you," she said.

"What is?" he asked.

"Not wanting any extra attention. I bet you wish sometimes you were invisible." Although, it would be a crime for a boy so good-looking to ever be invisible.

"I'd rather be invisible than have to carry books in a backpack like some fifth-grade dweeb," he said.

"It's not like you usually carry that many books," Angelita observed.

"I've got a lot of catching up to do," Kennin said, shoving several thick textbooks into the backpack.

"Since when do you care about catching up?" Angelita asked.

Kennin held her with those piercing dark eyes, and for a moment Angelita worried that she'd made him angry. But then he grinned. "Don't believe everything your brother says about me."

"Oh?" Angelita said. "And what do you think he says?"

"That I'm some kind of goof-off slacker."

"In school, or life in general?" she teased.

"What do you think?" Kennin asked.

"Maybe that's not what my brother says," Angelita said. She heard the teasing lilt in her voice but was unable to stop herself. Whenever they were alone and talking like this, it just seemed to happen naturally.

Suddenly Kennin hung his head, and the mood changed. "I'm still really sorry about the car. I mean it."

Angelita understood. But as much as she missed the 240 SX, she missed his lighthearted banter even more.

"It wasn't your fault," she said.

He lifted his head. "Any idea what would cause the wheel to break like that?"

She shook her head. "I've stayed up more than one night wondering."

For a moment they were both lost in thought. Kennin suspected that she was thinking back to the day of the crash. Earlier at school things had been tense. In the band room, it seemed like Kennin had blown her off for Mariel, but later he'd said that things weren't what they'd seemed. And then, just before the last tsuiso, they'd kissed. And that, except for the visit to the hospital, was the last time she'd seen him.

Kennin broke the silence. "So I hear you're graduating in December."

The lines between her eyes deepened. She'd only decided a few days before. "Tito told you?"

"Yeah."

"If I declare residency there I can qualify for the in-state tuition. It's the only way I can afford to go."

"Then you should do it," Kennin said. "California's got

one of the best state university systems in the country."

Angelita nodded. They both knew it was the right thing to do, but part of her wished he'd ask her not to go. But if he did ask, what would she do?

5

It wasn't until Kennin got to the cafeteria that he realized he had another problem. As long as he was on crutches, there was no way to carry a lunch tray. He glanced at his regular table near the window. Tito wasn't there.

"You look puzzled." Mariel appeared out of the crowd wearing a loose white blouse and tight jeans. She gave him her coyest smile.

"Trying to figure out how to get lunch," he replied.

"Simple," Mariel said. "I'll get it for you."

Kennin looked at the table where Chris Craven and the other gearheads normally sat. While Chris usually didn't sit with Mariel at lunch, Kennin had a feeling the guy wouldn't be too keen on seeing them together. But Chris wasn't with the gearheads.

Tito was.

"If you're looking for Chris, he's not here today,"

Mariel said. "Not that it would make any difference."

"So you've said before," Kennin replied. He was actually more curious about what Tito was doing at the gearhead table. "Only it seems sometimes that Chris would disagree."

"That I'm helping an injured person get lunch?" Mariel said innocently.

Was it strange to see Tito sitting with the gearheads? He was definitely friendly with some of them, like Mutt and Megs, but then there was Ian, who had a major problem with anyone who wasn't Anglo.

"Hello?" Mariel said.

Kennin looked back at her.

"So what were you planning on having?" she asked.

"They serving fries today?" Kennin asked.

"Tater Tots," said Mariel.

Kennin winced slightly. That wasn't his favorite meal. "Guess they'll have to do."

"And?" Mariel said.

"That's it."

"Tater Tots for lunch? Now that sounds like a healthy, well-balanced meal," Mariel said.

Kennin just shrugged.

"You're looking a little thin since the crash," Mariel said, putting her hands on her hips. "Why don't I treat you to something?"

Kennin was hungry, and he could rarely afford to treat

himself to a full lunch. Mariel smiled knowingly. "Okay, go sit. I know what to do."

Kennin sat down at an empty table and propped the crutches beside him. Over at the gearhead table, Tito glanced at him, then looked away. A few minutes later Mariel arrived carrying a tray with a chicken burrito, a baked potato, green peas, a salad, and peach slices.

Kennin thanked her. The food sitting inches from his face proved irresistible. Until that moment he hadn't realized how hungry he was. Or maybe he'd just gotten used to being hungry. Anyway, once he started to eat, it seemed like nothing could stop him.

"Somehow I don't think Tater Tots would have done the job," Mariel said with a smile when Kennin had finished.

"That was great," Kennin said, dabbing his lips with a paper napkin. "Thanks."

"Guess the hospital food wasn't gourmet?" Mariel asked.

"It wasn't bad," Kennin said.

Mariel scowled. "You mean, compared to what you usually eat?"

Kennin shrugged.

"I hear you live alone," Mariel said.

"With my sister," said Kennin.

"Does she go to school?"

Kennin shook his head.

"She works?"

"In entertainment," Kennin said.

"Where're your parents?" Mariel asked.

Kennin made a gesture with his hands. He didn't want to appear impolite, but he didn't enjoy being interrogated.

"I've also heard you're kind of private," Mariel said. Her eyes were lively and bright and she had an engaging way of chatting. The top three buttons of the white blouse were open, and Kennin had to fight to keep his eyes from wandering when she leaned forward.

"Who are you hearing all this from?" Kennin asked.

"Various people."

"I didn't think I was such a topic of conversation."

Mariel raised a doubtful eyebrow. "You sure? Or is the mysteriousness just a way of keeping people interested?"

"There's a difference between being mysterious and not wanting to talk about certain things," Kennin said. "Everyone has things they don't like to talk about."

"Okay, what *do* you like to talk about?" Mariel asked.

"Cars."

"Even after that crash?" Mariel asked.

Kennin shrugged. "Stuff happens."

"Have you heard about the new drifting team the Babylon might start?" Mariel asked.

"I know there's been some talk," Kennin said.

"A bunch of guys are going to try out."

"Including Chris?" Kennin asked.

"Of course," said Mariel.

"You must be happy for him," Kennin said.

Mariel rolled her eyes. "If Chris Craven ever wants to have a steady girlfriend, he's going to have to figure out that women require more attention than cars."

"You can't just fill the tank and expect them to go anywhere you want?" Kennin joked.

Mariel smiled back. "I have a feeling you know better than that. And I bet you also know that when it comes to women, unlike cars, you don't have to ask the owner's permission before you take one for a spin."

"I'll keep it in mind," Kennin said.

"So what about you?" Mariel asked. "I mean, in terms of the Babylon drift team?"

"Hard to say." Kennin rapped his knuckles against the cast. "It's a little soon to be thinking about it, you know?"

Kennin wasn't sure Mariel had heard him. Suddenly her face hardened as she stared past him. "What?" she snapped.

Kennin twisted around. Ian was standing behind him, with his baseball cap on backward, as usual. He was a short, stocky red-haired guy on the football team with Chris, and liked to think of himself as a big gangsta thug.

"Look who's back," Ian said with a smirk.

"Get lost," Mariel snapped.

"Now, now," Ian said in a teasing, scolding voice, "I don't think Chris would want to hear you talk that way."

"I don't give a crap what Chris wants to hear," Mariel said. "I said, get lost, loser."

Ian winced slightly. Kennin noticed that the cafeteria had grown quiet. People were listening and watching. Tito and a couple of the other guys from the gearhead table had gotten up and were coming over.

"You're calling me a loser?" Ian spit. "Look who you're sitting with."

"Crashing isn't losing," Mariel shot back. "Besides, I seem to recall that he handled you pretty easily, both in a car and with his fists."

Ian's face began to flush. "You ever notice how few races this guy actually finishes?" he said contemptuously.

"That's funny," Mariel replied. "Every time he races against *you* he not only finishes, but wins."

By now Tito, Megs, and the others had arrived. A couple of guys heard what Mariel said and chuckled.

Ian's face was bright red. "That's bull. The first time he didn't even drift. And the second time he frickin' tried to run me into a solid rock wall."

"Excuses, excuses," Mariel said with a dramatic sigh and a wave of her hand, as if she'd heard it all before. "Let me ask you something, Ian. Have you ever actually won a drift battle? Because I can't remember one."

"You know, Chris isn't going to be real happy when I tell him you bought gook-a-look here a three-course lunch," Ian shot back.

Kennin placed his hands flat on the table and tried to launch himself up, but the long stiff cast on his left leg hit the edge. He almost lost his balance and had to grab the table to steady himself.

Ian laughed. "What are you tryin' to do, Chinaboy? Kung fu with a cast? Hey, maybe they call it cast fu!"

If Ian thought he was going to get some laughs, he was wrong. The crowd around him was silent.

"Take that back," Kennin warned him.

"Or what?" Ian said.

Instead of answering, Kennin reached for his crutches, sliding one under each arm. By now the cafeteria had gone dead silent.

"Kennin, don't," Mariel said.

"You gotta be kidding," Ian sputtered nervously, glancing at the guys around him. "You think I'm gonna fight a guy with a cast and crutches? I'd look like an idiot."

"I have news for you," Kennin said, planting the crutches on the floor and inching toward him. "You already look like an idiot. I'm tired of telling you to cut that racist crap. You take it back right now, or else."

Ian twisted his head from side to side. "You hear that?" he asked the guys around them. "He's calling me out. I'm not starting this, he is."

No one answered.

"Kennin, stop," Mariel said.

But Kennin didn't stop.

"You don't stand a frickin' chance," Ian said.

"He's right, Kennin," Tito said.

But Kennin still didn't stop.

"Come on, guys," Ian practically pleaded. "Someone call this nutcase off before he gets hurt."

No one called Kennin off.

"Okay, Chinaboy, you asked for it." As Ian started to lift his fists, Kennin flipped one of the crutches around and shoved the wide end into Ian's stomach like a battering ram.

"Oof!" Ian let out a grunt and doubled over.

Kennin was raising the crutch over his head with every intention of bringing it down hard on Ian's back when Megs grabbed it.

"Don't, Kennin," he said. "You'll get expelled."

At that moment Kennin didn't care, but Megs held the crutch tight and wouldn't let go. Ian was still doubled over, gasping for breath. He looked like he'd had the wind knocked out of him.

"What's going on here?" It was Mr. Winchester, Kennin's geometry teacher.

"Nothing," Tito quickly said.

Mr. Winchester, who had the world's worst comb-over and some of the bushiest gray eyebrows ever, raised one of those eyebrows dubiously. "Tito, it's obvious something is going on. Ian's doubled over, and it appears that Kennin wants to use that crutch in a non-medically-approved way."

"Guess you could say something *was* going on, Mr. Winchester, but it's over now," said Mariel.

Holding his stomach, Ian slowly straightened up. His face was still red, and he was still breathing hard.

"You okay?" Mr. Winchester asked.

He nodded.

"Where do you usually sit?" Mr. Winchester asked.

Ian pointed at the gearhead table over by the windows.

"Why don't you and your friends go back over there?" Mr. Winchester said. "I see you on this side of the cafeteria again and there'll be a problem."

Ian shot Kennin an angry look and muttered something Kennin couldn't quite understand.

"That's enough," Mr. Winchester said sternly. "Get back to your table."

Ian and the others left, but Mr. Winchester stayed. He crossed his arms and studied Kennin. "Don't see much of you in class these days."

"I have to take a bus to school in the morning," Kennin said. "Sometimes it's late."

"You work after school?" Mr. Winchester asked.

Kennin nodded.

"How late?"

"Midnight, usually."

"And then you have to take a bus home from there?"

"Yes, sir."

Mr. Winchester made a face. "There's no point in coming

to school on five hours' sleep, Kennin. Studies have proven that the brain can't retain information on that little amount of rest."

Kennin raised his hands in a helpless gesture.

"You really have to work?" Mr. Winchester asked. "It's not like you're doing it just for a hot set of rims?"

"I had to buy him lunch today," Mariel said.

"Well, try your best to get to class, Kennin," Mr. Winchester said. "I can cut you some slack, but you're going to have to make up what you missed and show up a little more often."

He walked away. Kennin sat down again with Mariel. Her eyes were wide and gleaming. "Tell me something," she said. "Is there anything you're actually afraid of?"

"Plenty," Kennin replied.

Broken leg or not, Kennin had to get back to work. After school he caught a bus downtown to the Babylon Casino and hobbled into the valet parking garage on his crutches. Tito, in his khaki car-washing uniform, looked up from a silver BMW 760Li he was washing.

"What are you doing here?" he asked.

Not the friendliest greeting, Kennin thought. "What do you think?"

"You gonna wash cars with a broken leg?"

"Unless someone pays me not to."

Tony, the head of valet parking, came out of the office to greet him.

"Hey, look who's here!" Tony gave Kennin a hug. "How's the leg?"

"Still there," Kennin said. "How's the kid?"

"Great," Tony said. "Getting bigger. Eats a lot. Sleeps

through the night. My wife keeps telling me we got lucky. All I know is with the price of diapers, I sure don't feel lucky." He looked at the cast. "You sure you can work?"

"No choice," said Kennin. "Thanks for not giving my job away."

"You kiddin'?" Tony patted him on the back. "No way. Go ahead and change."

Kennin went into the locker room and changed into his khaki uniform. The left leg of the pants barely fit over the cast. Back out in the garage he joined Tito beside the BMW.

"You see what they're doing out back?" Tito asked.

Kennin shook his head. He dipped a brush into a bucket of soapy water and started to scrub the BMW's wheels.

"You know that empty lot they use when there's an overflow crowd?" Tito asked. "They're turning it into a drift track."

Kennin nodded silently.

"So what do you think?" Tito asked.

"Feels a little soon to be thinking about that," Kennin said.

"I'm not so sure you can wait," Tito said. "Ever since the crash, the talk's been about moving the scene off the street. Not just because of the cops, but the whole danger thing. Seeing what happened to you kind of shook everyone up."

"I bet," Kennin said.

"So the timing's kind of fortunate," Tito went on. "No one wants to run tsuisos on the street anymore, and now Mercado wants to make it legitimate. That can only be good for us."

"Oh yeah?" Kennin said.

"Sure," Tito said. "Think of the opportunity. Legitimate racing. Sponsorships. Teams. Real money. Better cars. Safer conditions. Everyone comes out a winner."

They'd finished soaping the BMW. Tito picked up a hose and started to rinse the car down. At the same time he moved closer to Kennin and lowered his voice. "I'm telling you, Kennin, this is our shot. Just between you and me, I've had it with this car-washing crap. The only reason I haven't quit this job is because it keeps me close to the action and close to Mercado. This is gonna be the best thing that ever happened to drifting around here."

Maybe, Kennin thought. But he also remembered something his father once said: *If it sounds too good to be true, it usually is.*

Their shift usually ran from four p.m. until midnight. The offer of a free car wash with valet parking ended at eleven thirty p.m. Just after midnight Tito and Kennin were in the locker room changing back into their street clothes when they heard the high-pitched whine of Mike Mercado's Ferrari Scaglietti out in the garage. Next came the heavy, soft thud as one car door shut, then another.

"Mercado's just getting to work," Tito said, shaking his head as if it was hard to believe. "The casino never sleeps."

A moment later the locker room door opened and Mike Mercado, the owner of the casino, and Derek Jamison, his right-hand man, stepped in. Mercado was a short man with a gleaming bald head. He was dressed in a dark suit, shirt, and tie. Derek was heavyset with a mop of unkempt black hair, dressed as usual in a wrinkled jacket. Both men stopped and looked around at the dented green lockers, and the pictures of cars and babes torn from magazines and pasted to the walls.

"This could be the one room in my casino I've never been in," Mercado said.

"This and the ladies' powder room," Derek corrected him.

Mercado turned his attention to Kennin's leg. "How is it?"

"Getting better," Kennin said.

"Guess it shows you the danger of racing in the street," Derek said.

Kennin wasn't sure it showed him that at all, but he wasn't going to argue.

"I assume you've heard that Derek is developing a drift team," Mercado said. "As soon as you feel up to it, we'd like you to join."

Kennin looked down at his leg and back at the casino owner. "I appreciate that, sir."

Mercado turned to leave, with Derek right behind him.

"Uh, Mr. Mercado," Tito suddenly blurted.

The casino owner stopped. "Yes?"

"Sir, I'd just like to point out that the foundation of any competitive automotive venture of this magnitude has got to be the tech crew," Tito said, using more big words in that sentence than he'd probably used in the entire past year. "I'd like to offer my services in that regard."

Mercado's forehead furrowed slightly. "And you are . . . ?"

"Tito Rivera." Tito offered his hand and Mercado shook it. "We met in your office about a month ago, remember?"

From the expression on Mercado's face, it was obvious that he didn't remember. But Tito didn't seem to notice that.

"You should speak to Derek about tech matters," Mercado said. "I'm sure he'll be interested."

Tito eagerly turned to Derek, who raised his hand, palm forward. "I'll keep it in mind, kid. Don't you worry. But right now I gotta run." He and Mercado left.

"You see?" Tito said as soon as the men left the locker room. "If I wasn't still doing this stupid job, that wouldn't have happened. Those guys aren't thinking about tech right now. They're too busy with the track and the drivers. But one of these days they're gonna figure out that without tech support, the whole thing's gonna fall apart. And that's when they're gonna remember me."

Kennin looked at the clock on the wall. It was after midnight and he still had a forty-five-minute bus trip home, and then school the next morning. He slid his crutches under his arms, and he and Tito left the locker room. Out in the garage the valet office was empty.

"Where's Tony?" Kennin asked.

"He's been leaving early lately," Tito said. "He gave me a key so I can lock up."

Kennin gazed out toward Las Vegas Boulevard just as a familiar-looking yellow Corvette cruised by. Jack the jackass was driving and Shinchou was in the passenger seat. While Kennin couldn't hear what was being said, he could definitely see that Jack was shaking his head and gesturing angrily. Suddenly he reached over and slapped Kennin's sister. Kennin felt his stomach knot with anger. His first reaction was to run to the car. But on the crutches he wouldn't get close before the light changed.

He quickly hobbled to the valet parking office door and tried it. The knob didn't turn. He looked at Tito. "You said Tony gave you a key?"

"Yeah. Why?"

"Give it to me," Kennin said.

"You crazy?" Tito stammered.

Kennin had no time to waste. "Give it to me or I'll take it," he said in a way that left no doubt about his intentions.

"What are you gonna do?" Tito asked as he handed over the key.

Kennin didn't answer. He let himself into the office and grabbed the first set of keys off the board. They were on a BMW fob.

"Are you frickin' crazy?" Tito gasped as Kennin came out of the office. "You know what's gonna happen if you get caught? Not only will you get fired, but you'll never get on the drifting team."

At that moment Kennin's concerns were a lot more immediate than the drifting team.

"This is so wrong, dude," Tito said as he followed Kennin into the valet area. "Forget what'll happen to you. If they find out I let you have the key I'll get fired too."

There were half a dozen BMWs in the valet lot and Kennin didn't have time to try the keys on each one. He pressed the red panic button on the key fob. The lights on the silver 760Li started to flash and the alarm went off. Kennin quickly killed it and headed for the car.

"Oh no," Tito groaned. "This I don't believe. Tell me this isn't happening!"

With the long, straight cast on, it wasn't easy for Kennin to get into the BMW. He tossed his crutches in the back, moved the seat back, tilted it, and got in.

Vrrrrooooooom! The sedan started with a roar.

Screeech! The wheels spun in reverse, leaving tread and smoke as Kennin backed it out of the parking spot, then

shifted into forward. He stopped beside Tito and quickly lowered the window. "You coming?"

"Are you insane?!" gasped Tito.

Kennin started to bring the window back up.

"Wait!" Tito suddenly cried, and yanked open the passenger door.

7

With Tito in the passenger seat, Kennin wheeled the big sedan out of the parking lot and onto the street, just in time to see the yellow 'vette turn a corner up ahead.

"What are we doing?" Tito asked, breathing hard.

"Following someone." Kennin made the same turn as the 'vette. Inside the 760Li the instrument panel glowed orange and yellow.

"You know this thing has a V-12 engine?" Tito asked. "Know what this car costs? Hundred forty grand all in."

"I'll keep that in mind," Kennin said. The 'vette was a block ahead, going through an intersection just as the light turned yellow. Kennin dropped the hammer and the big sedan's V-12 tapped into its 440 horses and shot forward like a rocket.

"Whoa!" Tito gasped next to him as they were both pressed back into the soft leather seats.

They sailed through the intersection just as the light turned red. Half a block ahead, the 'vette pulled into a parking lot in front of a dimly lit motel called the Time Out. A flickering red neon sign said VACANCY. It was the kind of place where rooms rented by the hour, and the doors opened directly into the parking lot so visitors could come and go without passing the front desk. Kennin killed the Beemer's lights and pulled up to the curb.

"That the guy we're following?" Tito asked, pointing at the 'vette.

Kennin nodded. He had a feeling things were about to go from bad to worse. "I wish I had a phone."

"You're in luck." Tito dug into his pocket and pulled out a shiny new silver flip phone. Kennin didn't have time to ask where Tito had gotten it, or how he could afford it after losing all his money. He found the slip of paper Leon had given him and quickly punched in the number. He could tell from the way Leon answered that he'd woken him. Kennin apologized and then quickly explained why he'd called. Leon said he'd see what he could do.

"Who's Leon?" Tito asked as Kennin tossed the phone back to him.

"Tell you later," Kennin said. In the motel parking lot Jack got out of the 'vette and pulled open the passenger door.

"That's the guy?" Tito gasped.

"Yeah. Why? You know him?" Kennin asked.

"Uh, no, no, it's . . . just that he looks . . . I don't know, like someone you don't want to mess with."

Jack leaned into the passenger side of the 'vette and said something to Shinchou. Kennin couldn't make out the words, but the tone was angry and forceful. When Shinchou wouldn't get out of the car, Jack reached in and yanked her out. It took every ounce of Kennin's self-control not to leap out of the BMW.

"Whoa! What's that about?" Tito asked.

Kennin watched with simmering anger as Jack held Shinchou's arm tightly and led her toward the motel. They stopped under a light while Jack knocked on a door. Shinchou hung her head. The door was opened by a fat guy in a sleeveless T-shirt. He gave Shinchou a quick once-over and then nodded. Jack pushed Kennin's sister into the room. The door closed. Jack lit a cigarette and strolled back to the 'vette.

"Number nine," Kennin said.

"What?" said Tito.

"She went into room number nine."

"Who is she?"

"My sister," Kennin said.

Tito didn't answer. He and Kennin both had sisters, so he understood what Kennin must have been feeling at that moment.

"Here's what you're gonna do," Kennin said. "As soon as the guy in the cowboy hat gets in the 'vette and takes off, you—"

"He doesn't look like he's taking off anywhere," Tito said. Jack was leaning against the 'vette, smoking.

"Believe me, he will," Kennin said. "And when that happens, you go to room number nine and knock hard and keep knocking until the fat guy opens the door."

"Crap," Tito muttered.

"When the guy opens the door, you tell him if he doesn't let my sister go right now you're gonna call the cops."

"What if the guy wants to kick the shit out of me?" Tito asked.

"He won't," Kennin said.

"How do you know?" Tito asked.

"I know."

Tito wasn't buying it. "I'd really like to help you, dude, but there's no way I'm getting involved in this. It just ain't my problem."

The seconds were ticking past and Shinchou was in that room. Kennin didn't have time to argue. He held Tito steadily with his eyes. "Tito, I know why that wheel came off your sister's car the night I crashed. Someone loosened the lug nuts, and I'm pretty sure I know who did it."

Tito's eyes went wide and his face grew pale. "I—I don't know what you're talking about."

"Yes, you do," said Kennin. He gestured toward Jack, who was still leaning against the 'vette, smoking. "Maybe we should go ask him. And then we could go talk to Angelita."

Tito crossed his arms unhappily and slid down in the BMW's seat. "Dude, you don't know what happened."

"Tell me later." Kennin pointed at the motel. "Right now you're going in there and getting my sister. Wait for me back at the intersection."

Without a word, Tito opened the door and got out of the BMW.

"Hey." Kennin pointed at an empty beer bottle lying beside the curb. "Give me that, will you?"

Tito scowled and handed him the bottle. "Why?"

"It'll come in handy."

Jack was still leaning against the car, smoking. Kennin steered the BMW about fifty feet past the motel entrance, then stopped. With the motor running, he braced himself in the doorway, clutching the beer bottle in his right hand. Jack didn't notice him. Kennin hurled the bottle at the 'vette's windshield. He was sliding back into the BMW when he heard the sound of breaking glass.

"Hey!" Jack shouted.

By now Kennin was behind the wheel in the BMW, confident that Jack hadn't seen him. In the rearview mirror he watched as Jack jumped into the 'vette. Kennin gunned the big sedan and left a long strip of rubber and smoke.

The race was on.

The BMW had a 438 hp V-12 engine compared to the Corvette's 400 hp V-8, but the 'vette was lighter and quicker. Kennin knew he had to lose Jack in the turns. And why not have some fun, too? The BMW might have been an automatic, but with some deft heel and toe work Kennin could slide the car around corners with control and power. Tires squealing, he turned right at the next corner and sped down a dark street. In the rearview mirror, the 'vette skidded around the same corner, the rear end swinging too far around, almost doing a donut. Kennin swung left at the next corner and Jack followed, again oversteering and almost spinning out. Kennin actually had to slow down to wait for him to straighten the 'vette out before making the next right and flooring it. About halfway down the block he passed a row of plastic garbage cans and had an idea.

He quickly led Jack in the 'vette around the block again, and this time, when the garbage cans appeared in the Beemer's headlights, Kennin punched the accelerator hard. Just past the garbage cans he cut the wheel and yanked the e-brake, doing a 180 just as the 'vette came around the corner.

Kennin floored the BMW. Only now he was heading straight back at the 'vette.

Kennin aimed the left side of the Beemer's front bumper toward the left front fender of the 'vette. With less than fifty feet between the two speeding cars, Jack had a split-second choice: go head-on into the BMW or veer to the right.

The result was an explosion of garbage cans and white plastic garbage bags flying through the air as the 'vette plowed into them.

It was a small reward compared to what Jack had done to Shinchou, but Kennin could feel a smile creep across his lips. He quickly drove back to the intersection where he'd told Tito to wait with Shinchou. They were there, standing under a streetlight. Kennin skidded to a stop and pushed open the passenger-side door for his sister.

"Get in," he said.

His sister frowned. "Where'd you get this?"

"Tell you later," Kennin said. "Now get in fast before Jack gets here."

Tito got in the back while Shinchou got in the front. Kennin took off. Shinchou opened her bag and took out a cigarette.

"Better not," Kennin said. "Don't want the owner to know we borrowed his car."

Shinchou slid the cigarette back into the pack. "How'd you know I was there?"

"Just lucky," Kennin said.

Kennin's sister slid down in the seat and raked her fingers through her long black hair. Kennin glanced at Tito in the rearview mirror. "How'd it go?"

"Like you said," Tito said. "The guy was totally freaked. As we left he said something about his money."

"Guess he'll have to work that out with Jack," Kennin said.

Shinchou gave him a sour look. "Don't think you're doing me a favor. As soon as Jack finds me, I'm going to get it bad."

"Then he better not find you," Kennin said as he drove toward the south side of town.

Shinchou straightened slightly and became more alert. "What do you mean? Where are we going?"

"Someplace where Jack won't find you," her brother said.

"Maybe I *want* Jack to find me," Shinchou said.

Kennin glanced at his sister. She looked thin and pale, and the makeup around her eyes was smudged. Before she got involved with Jack, she'd never looked this bad. For a moment Kennin didn't understand why she'd want Jack to find her. Then he did. The crystal meth. He had what she craved.

A little while later they pulled up in front of a run-down wood-frame house. In the darkness Kennin noticed a couch on the porch. Sitting on the couch was a heavy woman wearing a ratty-looking housedress. Leon was sitting in a rocking chair next to her.

"What is this?" Shinchou asked nervously.

"A place where you can get help," Kennin said.

Shinchou stiffened. "I don't need help."

"Roll up your sleeve," Kennin said.

Shinchou slumped down in the seat. "No."

"You gotta go in there, Shin," Kennin said. "You can't go home. Not unless you want Jack shoving you into motel rooms with creeps until the morning they find your body in a Dumpster somewhere. You'll be safe here. No one will know where you are. And that woman knows how to help you."

Shinchou started to cry. Kennin reached over and softly stroked her hair. "Come on, sis. You know it's the right thing to do. You know Jack's just using you. The day he stops making money off you, you'll never see him again."

"I'm scared," Shinchou sobbed, wiping the tears off her cheeks. "What if he does find me?"

"He won't." Kennin looked over the seat at Tito. "Right, Tito?"

"Right," Tito replied.

"We're the only ones who know about this," Kennin told his sister while staring over the seat at Tito. "If Jack were ever to find out you were here, I'd know that there was only one person who could have told him."

Tito slid down in the backseat and nodded miserably.

Shinchou reluctantly got out of the car, and Kennin went with her. At the same time, the large woman and Leon came down the steps. The large woman, of course, was Sista Bertha, and Kennin realized at once that she had a special aura about her. She took Shinchou's hand and spoke softly to her, and in no time Kennin's sister was going up the stairs and into the house. Leon stayed behind.

"She'll be okay here," he said once Bertha and Shinchou went inside the house. "Like I told you before, it'll be up to your sister, but at least she'll have a chance."

"I don't know how to thank you," Kennin said.

"I told you, dawg," Leon said. "Someone did it for me. I'm just passing the good karma along." He glanced at the BMW. "Sweet ride."

"Not mine," Kennin said.

Leon nodded. "Better take it back to wherever it belongs before you're sorry."

"Will do."

They shook hands. Kennin got into the BMW and headed back toward the strip.

"Dude, too bad we have to bring this thing back, huh?" Tito said. Kennin didn't answer. He and Tito both knew Tito had some explaining to do regarding the tsuiso and Kennin's crash.

Tito gnawed on his thumbnail. The streets outside grew brighter with neon signs and thousands of lightbulbs. They were nearing the strip. Kennin drove and waited for Tito to speak.

Tito finally cleared his throat. "I swear, I didn't think you'd crash." The words sounded more like a mouse's squeak than a human voice.

"You loosened the lug nuts on the front wheel and thought I wouldn't crash?" Kennin asked in disbelief.

"I left them hanging by a thread," Tito said. "I figured you'd roll a few feet, the wheel would fall off, and that would be it. I almost had a frickin' heart attack when you went off the line and into the first turn."

The next question was obvious. "Why, Tito?"

"That Jack guy," Tito said. "The one back at the motel."

"How?" Kennin asked.

"He offered me five hundred bucks and I told him to go to hell," Tito said. "Then he threatened to break my leg with a baseball bat. Said he knew where I lived, where I worked, went to school, everything. I asked him how he knew all that stuff and he said you told him. Why'd you tell him?"

"I didn't," Kennin answered.

"Then how'd he know?" Tito asked.

Shinchou, Kennin thought. She'd probably told Jack all sorts of things in complete innocence. But Jack soaked everything in, knowing someday it might come in handy. "Did Jack have money on the tsuiso?"

"Yeah, I think so. A lot," Tito answered. "I mean, why else would he care, right? Jeez, dude, you don't know how sorry I am. When you broke your leg in that crash and my sister's car got totaled, I was ready to slit my own throat."

Kennin believed him. "You take the money?"

Tito stared at him. "You crazy? No frickin' way!"

"You should have," Kennin said. "If you were gonna do it anyway, why not? At least you'd have some money to help with my doctor bills and fixing your sister's car."

"Forget it," Tito said. "I wouldn't take that SOB's money if he paid me. Uh, wait, that doesn't make sense, but you know what I mean."

They turned onto the strip and rode along in silence, the lights of the casinos so bright it almost seemed like day. Ahead loomed the Babylon, a garish casino with huge fake gold and diamond decorations that were supposed to make the place look as if it were dripping in treasure. Tito snuck a peek at Kennin.

"So, uh, what do you say, Kennin? We friends again?"

Kennin glanced down at the long stiff cast that jammed the toes of his left leg against the firewall behind the pedals.

He believed Tito when he said he had no idea that loosening the lug nuts would cause so much pain and suffering. He could forgive him . . . up to a point. Trusting him again was a different story. "Sure, Tito, we're friends again."

The Babylon's parking garage had a rear exit ramp for drivers who preferred to depart on a back street rather than onto the strip. It was supposed to be one-way and exit only, but it was handy if you were returning a "borrowed" car. It was now close to two a.m. and the garage was quiet. Kennin pulled the BMW back into its spot, and he and Tito got out.

"Good thing we didn't get caught," Tito muttered as Kennin slid the crutches under his arms.

But the words were hardly out of his mouth when Kennin noticed the shiny black Hummer parked a few spaces away. The door opened, and Derek got out with a knowing smile on his face. Suddenly Kennin knew that Tito had spoken too soon.

9

"*You do that* often?" Derek asked.

"Park cars, sir?" Kennin replied innocently.

"Nice try. I'm talking about taking them out for a"—Derek glanced at his heavy gold and silver Rolex—"for a two-hour joyride."

Kennin scuffed his right foot against the garage floor. "No, sir, I've never done that before."

"It wasn't a joyride," Tito blurted. "Kennin's sister—"

"Shut up, Tito," Kennin snapped, then looked up at Derek. "I'm sorry, sir, it'll never happen again."

"Know what would happen if Mr. Mercado found out about this?" Derek asked.

"He'd break my other leg?" Kennin asked.

Derek smiled. "Smart boy. You read my mind."

"May I continue reading it, sir?" Kennin asked.

"Sure, let's see what you come up with," Derek said.

"My guess is you're not going to tell him about this, but you're not going to let us forget it either."

Derek looked down at Kennin's cast. "How soon before you're ready to drive again? I mean, *without* the cast."

"What makes you think I'll want to drive again?" Kennin asked back.

Derek glanced at the silver 760Li. "That's what I call a bad bluff, kid. Now listen up. You may be a good drifter, but you're not the only guy around who knows how to slide a car sideways. This thing catches on, we could be talking some serious money. And from what I hear, you could use a few extra dollars right now."

"Suppose I think about it?" Kennin said.

"Sure, go ahead," Derek said. "Just don't take too long. The train leaves the station whether or not you're on board."

Derek turned and climbed back into the Hummer. The big black SUV started up with a low rumble and pulled out of its spot.

Kennin started down the ramp on his crutches.

"I don't get it," Tito said, following him. "Why didn't he bust us?"

"That's not the way it works in this town," Kennin answered.

"Then how does it work?" Tito asked.

"He knows we owe him," Kennin said. "When the right time comes, he'll want to collect."

o   o   o

At lunch the next day, for the first time since the crash, Kennin and Tito sat together at their regular table by the cafeteria windows. Across the cafeteria Chris and Ian sat with Megs and Mutt and a bunch of other gearheads. Meanwhile, Mariel and her crowd of hot, popular girls and wannabes occupied a table in the middle of the room. They were serving Tater Tots again, and without Mariel treating, Kennin was back to his all-potato lunch.

"So whatever happened to Jack last night?" Tito asked with a yawn. They'd both gotten around three hours of sleep.

"He ran into some garbage," Kennin said.

Tito nodded and propped his head on his hand while he ate.

"What do you hear from Cousin Raoul these days?" Kennin asked. Tito's cousin was the one who'd actually boosted the GTO that Detective Neilson was so hot to nail Kennin for.

"Not much," Tito said.

"He still in the gardening business?"

"As far as I know," Tito said. "Why, you want a job cutting lawns?"

"I need a ride to the hospital this afternoon," Kennin said. "To get the cast taken off."

"I'll give him a shout." Tito flipped open the shiny silver cell phone, made the call, and left a message: "Hey,

Raoul, it's Cousin Tito. Got a favor to ask. Give me a yell, okay?" He snapped the phone shut.

"New phone?" Kennin asked.

"Check it out." Tito held it up and snapped a shot of Kennin, then handed him the phone. Kennin studied the shot that Tito had just taken. Mariel was right. His face did look thinner. It was strange how you might not notice it in a mirror, but the camera didn't lie. Kennin leaned forward, aimed the camera at the diamond stud in Tito's ear, and took a shot.

"So you noticed," Tito said with a grin.

Kennin nodded, but kept what he was thinking to himself—that for a kid who'd lost all his money betting on the tsuiso and refused to take any money from Jack, Tito sure was buying himself some nice things.

"So, uh, if I can't get hold of Raoul, how are you going to get to the hospital?" Tito asked.

It was a good question. Shinchou was at Sista Bertha's, and Angelita's 240 SX was trashed. Unless . . .

"Your sister hasn't found another ride, has she?" he asked.

Tito's face went stony. "We had a deal, remember? You said you'd leave her alone."

"I'm not asking for her hand in marriage, Tito," Kennin said. "Just a ride to the hospital. Which reminds me, how did you and she get there that time you came to visit?"

"Sometimes my mom lets her use her car," Tito said.

"If you don't want her around me, how come she came to the hospital?" Kennin asked.

"Because she wanted to," Tito said. "Wasn't like I could stop her. It was her car you got hurt in. I guess she felt responsible."

"Jeez." Kennin shook his head in disbelief.

"What?" Tito asked.

"You loosen the lug nuts, which causes me to break my leg while your sister's car gets completely trashed. And who winds up feeling responsible? Angelita."

Tito winced. "I told you I didn't think that would happen."

"Hey." Mariel sat down beside Kennin. The scent of her perfume filled his nostrils. She was wearing a tight, low-cut pink top and tight jeans. Tito was staring.

"Ahem." Kennin cleared his throat and Tito looked up, his face coloring.

"Back to Tater Tots for lunch, I see," Mariel said.

Kennin shrugged.

"How's the leg?" Mariel said.

"Funny you should ask," said Tito.

"It's nothing," Kennin quickly said.

Mariel gave Tito a puzzled look.

"He needs a ride to the hospital this afternoon so he can get the cast off," Tito said.

"I'll find someone," Kennin said.

"You just did," said Mariel.

10

Mariel said she'd meet him on the front steps after school. Kennin skipped out of study hall early and sat down to wait. When the bell rang, the doors swung open and kids started to stream out. Kennin pushed himself up off the steps and onto his crutches and hobbled off to the side so he wouldn't get trampled.

"Hey, you."

Kennin turned and found Angelita with her arms filled with books. Her black hair was brushed out and she was wearing makeup and looked great.

"You don't usually go home this way," Kennin said.

"I know," said Angelita. "Tito told me to meet him here. I don't know why."

Kennin smiled bitterly to himself. He knew exactly why Tito wanted his sister to be on the front steps when school ended.

"Have you seen him?" Angelita asked.

"I have a feeling he'll be taking his time," Kennin said.

The faint lines on Angelita's forehead deepened, but she didn't press the question. Instead she asked, "So how are you?"

"Better, thanks."

She nodded at the cast. "When does it come off?"

"Funny you should ask," Kennin said. "In about an hour."

"After only a month?" Angelita said. "That fast?"

"I'm tired of it," Kennin said. "Doctor said it could come off. Though he'd rather wait."

"Oh." Angelita scowled.

An awkward moment passed. Whenever she was near him, Angelita felt torn. She had a month to go before she could graduate and move to California. Everyone agreed it was the best thing for her. Kennin hardly came to school and seemed to have no other ambition than driving as fast as possible. The two of them didn't make sense together. Angelita knew it would be best if she steered clear of him.

Mariel came out the front doors. When she saw Kennin, a big smile appeared on her face. She brushed past Angelita and touched Kennin lightly on the arm. "Ready?" she asked.

Kennin gave Angelita one last look. But her eyes were downcast and she didn't see.

"Here. I'll take your bag," Mariel said, picking up his backpack. She held it in one hand and placed her other hand on Kennin's arm, as if he needed help getting down the steps. Kennin knew it was just for show.

Mariel's IS300 was parked halfway down the block. When they got there, Mariel opened the door for him. Kennin tossed the crutches in the back, then angled the cast in and eased himself into the passenger seat.

"Thanks for doing this," he said when Mariel got into the driver's seat.

"My pleasure," she replied, and pulled away from the curb. The IS300 was a peppy little beast, and Mariel quickly shifted through the gears to third.

"The clinic's across town and it's a real pain getting on and off buses with this cast," Kennin said.

"You don't have to explain," Mariel said, and gestured to the LCD screen for the navigation system, which displayed a color map of Las Vegas. "Touch the screen where you want to go."

Kennin pressed his finger against the screen and an electronic voice instructed Mariel to make a left turn in two hundred feet.

"What happened to your Saab?" Kennin asked. Before the IS300, Mariel had driven a Saab convertible.

"The lease ran out," Mariel said. "The Swedish don't understand what it's like to live in a place where the average summer temperature is more than a hundred degrees. The black convertible top felt like a frying pan, so I decided to get a sedan."

"You picked well," Kennin said, admiring the instrument cluster, the leather seats, and the five-speed manual shift.

"So how's the 240 SX?" Mariel asked.

"Totaled," Kennin answered.

"What a shame," said Mariel. "I was sure you'd beat Chris that night."

They rode in silence for a while, Kennin thinking about what Mariel had just said.

"Can I ask you a personal question?" he finally said.

"Okay," said Mariel.

"Why are you so down on him?"

"Simple. He doesn't have a clue about how to treat a girl. To him we're just sex objects and arm candy."

"Ever tell him that?" Kennin asked.

"About a thousand times. He just doesn't get it." She swiveled her head and smiled at him. "You, on the other hand, seem to understand what a girl needs."

Kennin didn't answer. The computer voice in the navigation system told Mariel to prepare for a right turn in five hundred feet.

"Still think I'm playing you just to get Chris's attention?" Mariel asked.

"Why shouldn't I think that?" Kennin replied.

"Because maybe it's not true," said Mariel.

Kennin found that hard to believe. Chris Craven was the quarterback of the football team, drove a hot car, had plenty of money, and would be going to college next year. What wasn't to like? Meanwhile, Kennin spotted the beige concrete exterior of the hospital ahead of them on the right.

"That's it," he said.

They parked and went into the orthopedic outpatient clinic. With a medical resident watching, a nervous young blond medical student cut the cast off, using a small saw with a round blade. The student kept looking over her shoulder at the resident for approval.

"Just cut the stupid thing off already," the resident snapped impatiently.

"You're not instilling much confidence," said Mariel, who'd come into the room with Kennin.

"People pay for confidence," the resident replied wryly. "Your friend here gets to be a guinea pig."

The cast came off, and the accompanying odor made both Kennin and Mariel wrinkle their noses.

"Don't worry," said the resident. "It's just the accumulated dead skin. It'll go away as soon as you wash the leg."

They gave him a cane and a booklet of exercises for his leg, then sent him on his way. Kennin couldn't help but appreciate Mariel for staying with him the whole time, and even dealing with the smell from his leg, when she could have stayed in the waiting room and read *People* magazine. Maybe she wasn't just playing him to get Chris's attention.

"Where to now?" Mariel asked when they were back in the IS300.

"The Babylon," Kennin said.

"The doctor said you could go back to work?" Mariel asked, surprised.

"He didn't say I couldn't," Kennin replied.

"You don't want to give yourself a day off?"

"Can't afford it," Kennin said. That much was true, but he also didn't want to ask her to drive him home. The fewer people who knew where he lived, the better.

Mariel, who got a new car every time the lease on the old one ran out, mulled over what he'd just said. "Did you ever tell me what the deal was with your parents?"

Kennin hadn't. He appreciated Mariel's help, but he didn't want her pity. Telling her that his mother was dead and his father was doing time in the federal prison camp at Nellis Air Force Base was more information than she needed.

"They're back in California," he lied.

"Then why are you and your sister here?" Mariel asked.

"It's a long story," said Kennin.

"One I'm not gonna hear, right?" Mariel said.

They stopped in front of the Babylon. Before Kennin could get out of the car, Tito rushed out of the garage wearing his khaki car-washing uniform. He seemed excited, but slightly confused.

"Hey," he said to Kennin, but his eyes were on Mariel.

"Mariel just took me to get my cast off," Kennin explained.

"You're just in time," Tito said. "Chris is trying out the track."

From a distance came the high-pitched whine of a turbo-charged SR20DET. In the Lexus, Kennin became alert.

Tito grinned. "Music to your ears, right?"

Kennin felt an instant yearning to see the car. No matter how hard he tried to resist, deep down he wanted to see the track and what Chris was doing.

"Oh yeah, I see it!" Tito chuckled and turned to Mariel. "You see it in his eyes? This guy's got transmission fluid in his veins."

Kennin pushed open the Lexus's door and grabbed the cane from the back. He turned to Mariel. "Thanks for the ride. I really appreciate it."

"Hold on," she said. "I'm going with you."

11

While Mariel parked the Lexus, Tito gave Kennin a curious look. "Okay, here's what happens next," he said. "I'll say, 'What's that about?' and you'll say, 'Nothing,' and I'll say, 'Mr. Mysterious again,' and you'll just shrug. The silent routine is getting old, dude. Maybe it's time to come up with something new."

"I thought you'd be happy," Kennin said, and nodded at the Lexus. "If I'm with her, I'm not messing with your sister."

"Right," Tito replied. "Let's keep it that way."

Mariel got out of the Lexus and walked toward them. Tito slapped his hands together. "All right! Let's go!"

They went around the parking garage toward the overflow lot behind the casino. The squealing and screeching of tires and the whine of the engine grew louder.

"Does it sound like he's having fun, or what?" Tito asked eagerly.

Kennin saw white smoke rising in the air before he saw either the car or the course. Workers had erected a temporary plywood fence while they'd turned the lot into a track. Next he smelled the oily scent of recently laid asphalt. They found an opening between the plywood sheets and went in.

"Oh, man!" Tito groaned loudly at the sight. Spread before them were four acres of smooth, glistening black asphalt. Workers with a tall crane were installing a bank of lights on one of four towers designed to illuminate the track at night. A winding, overlapping course had been laid out using orange cones, and Chris's shimmering red 240 SX *Slide or Die* was drifting sideways in a storm of smoke and screeching thunder.

"I'm frickin' dying watching him," Tito moaned. "He's got boost and pushing four hundred rwhp!"

A group of people were standing about fifty yards away, near several piles of tires. Kennin recognized Ian, Derek, Driftdog Dave, and Mutt and Megs. Parked on the tarmac behind them in what resembled a pit area were Ian's white Toyota Cressida and Driftdog's Nissan 180 SX turbo splotched gray and black with body putty and primer.

A moment later Chris finished the course and rolled *Slide or Die* to a stop in front of the group. He got out and pulled off his helmet, then stared for a long moment at Kennin and Mariel. He turned to the others and started to talk, mostly to Derek. Kennin was too far away to hear what he was saying.

Driftdog spotted them and came over. He was a tall guy with long brown hair pulled back into a ponytail, and a scar through his left eyebrow. Earlier in the fall he'd blown the 180 SX's engine in a tsuiso against Chris. The car had caught fire and Kennin had helped him get out before he got seriously burned.

Driftdog gave Kennin a high five. "Hey, how's the leg?"

"Just got the cast off," Kennin said.

"Way to go," Driftdog said.

"You been out on this yet?" Kennin asked, nodding at the course.

"Yeah, just killed a set of tires," Driftdog said. "What a frickin' blast."

"How's the surface?" Kennin asked.

"Still sticky," said Driftdog. "Makes it a little harder to break free. But in a couple of weeks it's gonna be awesome. You want to take my car around the track a few times?"

Ever since he'd "saved" Driftdog, the guy had been trying to pay him back. "It's a nice offer," Kennin said. "But my left leg's still kind of weak. I have to build it back up before I start working a clutch."

"Gotcha," Driftdog said. "But when the time's right, you let me know."

Meanwhile, the group over by *Slide or Die* was still talking.

"What do you think they're gabbing about?" Tito asked.

"Mostly the track layout," Driftdog said. "They've been fiddling with it all afternoon."

Sure enough, Megs and Mutt walked out on the track and started to move the orange cones around, widening the apex in one of the curves. While Ian headed for the white Cressida, Chris joined Kennin, Tito, and Mariel. He glanced from Mariel to Kennin and back.

"Where you been?" he asked Mariel.

"I took a friend to get his cast off," Mariel replied.

Chris looked at Kennin. "You gonna drive again?"

"Not sure," Kennin replied.

"He will," Tito declared. "All he has to do is get his hands on a decent beater and you'll see."

An engine revved loudly behind them as Ian took off in the white Cressida. He entered the first curve with a big sideways slide and wound up doing a donut. The Cressida stalled in a cloud of white smoke. Ian quickly started it up, redlined the engine, and promptly turned another donut, this time plowing through half a dozen orange cones before stalling a second time. Starting up again, he took off for the next turn, creating a loud scraping sound.

"What's wrong with his car?" Mariel asked.

"Nothing," Kennin said. "He's just dragging two cones."

"Oh yeah." Tito grinned at the sight of the cones jammed under the Cressida.

Ian must have heard the noise, because he stopped in the middle of the track and got out of the car. Everyone watched from the pit area while he walked around the car, searching for the source of the scraping sound, which had stopped when the car stopped. Next he popped the Cressida's hood.

Finding nothing wrong, Ian got back into the car. No sooner did the car start to move than the loud scraping noise began. Once again Ian stopped, got out of the car, and walked around it for the second time, obviously mystified by the source of the noise.

"That's so phat!" Tito chuckled. "He can't figure it out!"

"Neither would you if you were out there," Chris muttered.

That was probably true, but it was still funny to watch Ian get back in the car and start to drive, only to stop as soon as the scraping began again. For the third time he searched for the source of the sound. Finally, he got back into the car and drove slowly back toward the pit with the dull sound of scraping still coming from under the car.

"Is this a tryout for the team?" Tito asked Chris.

Chris shook his head. "They just asked if anyone wanted to come over and try the track."

"What do you think?" Kennin asked.

Chris studied him for a moment, as if uncertain how to answer. Finally he said, "I'm not sure I like it. It's kind of like going back to where most of us started. Killing tires doing donuts in an empty parking lot. And it's mostly a first- and second-gear course. Kind of hard to get up any real speed. I guess the safety thing is pretty big right now, but I don't know about judged events. It's not the same as a tsuiso."

"But you could get sponsored," Tito said. "Think about a deal with Yokohama or Cooper and then never having to buy tires again."

Chris nodded thoughtfully, then turned to Mariel. "I'm finished here. Gonna put the street rubber back on and bounce. Want to go?"

Mariel looked at Kennin, then back at him. "I might want to stay."

Chris's face hardened, and once again he looked from Mariel to Kennin.

"You should go," Kennin said to Mariel. "I've got to get to work."

Mariel shrugged a shoulder, as if she didn't care one way or another. "My car's in the front," she told Chris. "I'll meet you there."

Chris and Driftdog walked back toward the pit. At the same time, Mariel, Tito, and Kennin headed for the parking garage.

"Don't take this the wrong way, *mi amigo*, but you're running out of time," Tito said to Kennin. "You gotta make up your mind about the team."

"Thanks for the advice," Kennin said. They got back to the parking garage. Tito went into the locker room, leaving Kennin and Mariel alone.

"I really appreciate that ride today," Kennin said.

Mariel's eyes darted left and right and Kennin could tell she had something on her mind. She took Kennin's hand and placed his palm against her cheek. Her eyes burrowed deep into his. "I meant what I said before," she said, slowly moving his hand down to her throat, and then lower. "About what a girl needs. Think about it."

A little after midnight Kennin caught the bus home. The city bus system was nicknamed the CAT, short for Citizens Area Transit. There usually weren't many people riding after midnight, and Kennin had gotten to know the driver, a woman named Sheila.

"Hey, you got the cast off!" she said when he climbed on, using the cane.

"Yeah." Kennin sat down in the first seat by the door.

"How's it feel?"

"Weak, but better without that heavy cast."

"Well, your timing's good," Sheila said.

"How's that?" Kennin asked.

"Looks like the CAT drivers are going on strike," Sheila said. "We've been working without a contract for almost a year and the union's had it."

The ride home could be pretty fast some nights, with Sheila passing empty bus stop after empty bus stop. Pretty soon they were near the Sierra Ne-Vue. Kennin got up.

Sheila gave him a concerned look. "How're you gonna get home from work at night if we go on strike?"

"Not a clue," Kennin answered.

"Well, good luck," Sheila said.

Kennin got off and started to limp on the cane toward the Sierra Ne-Vue. His left leg felt weak and had begun to throb. He'd just passed the dead brown palm trees at the entrance to the trailer park when he spotted a black Escalade parked outside his trailer. The car had twenty-inch custom rims. The black windows were partway down to let out cigarette smoke. Kennin knew who was inside.

He stopped in the dark, knowing he had two choices, and they both sucked: He could either not go home, which left him with no place else to go, or he could go home and face Jack and his goons. It had been a long day, and Kennin was tired. All he wanted to do was go to sleep. He limped toward the Escalade. When he got close, the passenger door opened and Jack the jackass got out.

"Where's my sister?" Kennin asked.

Jack stopped, obviously caught by surprise. Then he grinned. "Nice try, boy. Almost got me there."

"Tell me where she is or I'm going to the police," Kennin threatened.

Jack narrowed his eyes. "You're lying."

"I am frickin' serious," Kennin said. "First you got her with the loan sharking and stupid weekly vig. Then you got her on dope. The cops are gonna have a field day with you."

A guy the size of a sumo wrestler got out of the Escalade. Kennin had met him a few weeks ago when it had been Jack's turn to do the threatening. His nickname was Tiny and he had a shaved head and wore a thick silver chain with a medallion around his neck.

"Everything okay?" Tiny asked.

"Yeah, get back in the car," Jack barked, then turned to Kennin. "I wouldn't go to the cops if I was you."

"Give me one good reason why not," Kennin said.

"Because I don't know where she is," Jack said. "She's not at the club and she's not here."

Kennin glanced at the trailer. The windows were dark. "When was the last time you saw her?"

"Four or five days ago," Jack answered.

"Where?"

"The club."

He was lying. The last time Jack had seen Shinchou was when he left her in room nine at the Time Out motel. But Kennin couldn't reveal that without Jack figuring out who'd broken the windshield of his 'vette.

They'd reached a standoff. Kennin's thoughts raced as he tried to figure out if he could use this situation to his advantage. After all, Jack was the SOB who not only had messed up his sister, but also had forced Tito to loosen the lug nuts on Angelita's car.

"Your sister owes me a boatload of money. Sooner or later she's gonna show up, and when she does, believe me, boy, she's gonna pay." The jackass turned around and got into the Escalade. The lights flashed on and the SUV

rumbled out of the trailer park. Kennin watched the red tail-lights disappear into the passing traffic. He breathed a sigh of relief. Once again he'd managed to protect his sister. But there was a ton of money on the line, and sooner or later Jack and his goons would be back.

Kennin climbed up the loose cinder-block steps to the trailer. He unlocked the door, stepped inside, and turned on the lights. An envelope was lying on the floor just inside the doorway. Kennin tore it open. Inside was an eviction notice for nonpayment of rent. Kennin crushed the notice into a ball and shot it into the garbage can. Looked like he and his sister just couldn't catch a break.

12

 A week later the CAT drivers went on strike. Thanks to the major delays and cancellations on bus routes, Kennin didn't get to school until lunchtime.

"You're late," Tito said, while Kennin dumped some books and his jacket into his locker. Las Vegas might be sunny, but it wasn't always warm. At least not in early December. On the really chilly mornings Kennin wore a camouflage jacket over a hoodie.

"No kidding." Kennin closed his locker door and started toward the cafeteria.

"Where's the cane?" Tito asked, walking alongside him.

"Decided to try a day without it," Kennin answered. He'd been doing the exercises his doctor had suggested, and his leg felt stronger and steadier.

"They're starting the real tryouts for the Babylon Drift Team," Tito said. "You don't want to miss your shot."

Kennin wasn't so sure about that. And anyway, there was something else getting in the way. "I got a problem, Tito. It's spelled *n-o-c-a-r*."

"Nocar," Tito repeated. "Oh, no car?"

"Uh-huh."

"Maybe you can borrow one," Tito said.

"Sure, people are lining up to lend their cars to the guy who totaled your sister's 240 SX," Kennin said, not bothering to hide his bitterness.

Tito's face colored. The implication was obvious. When he'd loosened those lug nuts he'd done a lot more than trash his sister's car and break Kennin's leg. He'd also gone a long way toward destroying Kennin's reputation as a drifter. Tito hung his head.

"Dude, I told you I was sorry. That Jack guy was gonna break my frickin' legs. I didn't know what to do. I was scared."

Kennin believed him. Someone else might have handled the situation differently. Maybe they would have disappeared into the brush, or locked themselves in a car. Kennin didn't know what the exact circumstances had been. He just knew that Tito hadn't spent a lot of time around bad dudes and, as a result, tended to scare easily.

"If the buses are on strike, how're you gonna get to work after school today?" Tito asked.

"Don't know," Kennin said.

"You want, you can ride on the pegs of my bike," Tito offered.

The idea of getting to work on the pegs of Tito's BMX was less than thrilling, but at the moment Kennin didn't have a better idea. "Thanks, I'll think about it."

Later he was in the hall after English class when someone said, "Hey, no cane." He turned. Angelita was behind him, carrying an armload of books.

"First day without it," Kennin said.

"How's it feel?"

"A little shaky, that's all. I figure in a week or two it'll be good as new."

"You hear they've started the tryouts for the drifting team?" Angelita asked, giving him a searching look.

Kennin nodded. "Tito told me."

"And you're not interested?"

"Doesn't matter," Kennin said. "I've got no wheels."

"Didn't I notice a Corolla parked next to your trailer?" she asked.

"My sister's car?" Kennin said.

"It's an eighty-six, right?" Angelita said. "Rear wheel drive. You could swap in a supercharged 4agze. Turbo it and you'd have a twincharged ae86."

"It's not a simple drop-in," Kennin said. "You'd have to custom-fabricate a working throttle cable set up on the opposite side of the engine."

They stopped at Angelita's locker. Inside was a photo of Viggo Mortensen. The locker itself was neat and clean, the books stacked in an orderly fashion. As Angelita reached into her locker, a smile grew slowly on her lips. "I'm impressed. There aren't many guys around here who'd know that. What else?"

"Replace the suspension bushings because they're probably shot from age," Kennin said. "Throw in a full coilover suspension. Upgrade the brake system."

Angelita's smile became broader. "So what's stopping you?"

"Money," Kennin said. "It would take a lot. Second, the thing's a rusty piece of junk. Third, she'd never agree to let me drift it."

"Have you asked?"

"No."

"Suppose you did?"

"I have to think about it first," Kennin said.

"So maybe it's not just about the car?" Angelita asked.

Kennin didn't answer. The bell rang and the hall began to clear out.

"Don't you have to get to your next class?" Angelita asked.

"Study hall," Kennin said with a shrug. "You?"

"I've got a free," she said. "I'll walk with you."

They started down the hall, taking their time. "You know the other day, on the front steps," Kennin began to say.

"I know," Angelita quickly cut him off. "She was just giving you a ride to the hospital. To get the cast off."

"It was the only way I could get there," Kennin said.

"You don't have to explain," Angelita said. "I think I've figured out what's going on. My brother told you that you weren't good enough for me, and that made you mad."

Kennin didn't answer.

"He only did that because he loves me," Angelita said. "I know we rag on each other a lot, but that's just dumb brother and sister junk, you know?"

Kennin nodded. It was that way between him and Shinchou.

"I'll be the first one in my family to go to college," Angelita said. "That's a huge thing for us. Tito really wants me to go. What he really doesn't want is to see me mess up my life at the age of eighteen like our mom did. You can understand, right?"

"Yes," Kennin said.

"Frankly, I'd prefer my brother didn't stick his nose where it doesn't belong, but at least I understand why he does it."

Kennin wondered how understanding Angelita would be if she knew Tito had loosened those lug nuts.

"Guess you'll be leaving for California soon," he said.

Angelita nodded and stared at the hallway floor.

"Ever been there before?" Kennin asked.

"No."

"You won't believe it. I mean, a lot of it's kind of ugly,

like every place else," Kennin said. "But other parts . . . especially near the ocean . . . You gotta promise me you'll watch the sun set over the ocean. You can't imagine how beautiful it is. Out there people are so used to it, a lot of them don't even bother, but it's amazing. So you gotta promise me, okay?"

Angelita nodded but wouldn't look at him. She pulled a tissue out of her bag and dabbed her eyes.

"What's wrong?" Kennin asked.

"Nothing," she answered. "I just got something in my eye. That's all."

Kennin stopped outside his study hall. Angelita had finished dabbing her eyes, but they were still red. "You sure you're okay?" he asked.

"Yes," she said. "Whatever it was, I got it out."

"Later," Kennin said and went in.

Angelita watched him go. There'd been nothing other than tears in her eyes, of course. And they both knew it.

The day was over. Kennin was at his locker.

"Ready?" someone said.

He turned and found Tito.

"Oh yeah, can't wait," Kennin answered, picturing himself standing on the pegs of Tito's BMX bike while Tito pedaled through Las Vegas traffic.

"Hey, don't kid yourself," Tito said. "I get there faster on my bike than you do by bus."

Outside school, Tito's chrome BMX was chained to the bike rack. Kennin gazed wistfully down the block toward the bus stop, as if somehow a bus would magically appear.

"What's up?" It was Mariel in her red IS300, at the curb.

"On my way to work," Kennin said.

"Doesn't look like you're in a hurry," Mariel said.

"The buses are on strike," Kennin said.

"Then how are you going to get there?" she asked.

Tito unlocked his BMX and walked it over to Kennin. "Here we go, dude."

In the car, Mariel smiled. "You're going to work on *that*?"

"I sit on the seat and pedal while he stands on the pegs," Tito explained.

Mariel pursed her lips and swung her blond hair away from her face. "I'm going downtown. I could give you a ride."

"You sure?" Kennin asked.

"Are you whack?" Tito said, getting on the BMX. "Given the choice between my pegs and those wheels? I'll see you at the Babylon." He rode off down the sidewalk.

Kennin got into Mariel's car.

"Can I ask you a favor?" he said as she started to drive. "Could you be the one person today who doesn't ask me if I'm going to try out for the drift team?"

"Sure."

They drove in silence for a little while, and then Mariel

asked, "How are you getting to school if there's a bus strike?"

"The buses run. Just not that often," Kennin said. "If you wait long enough one comes."

"You weren't in Mr. Winchester's class this morning," Mariel said. "Of course, you're usually not there even when the buses do run. So what time did you get to school today?"

"End of fifth period."

Mariel turned and looked at him. "And how are you going to get home tonight after work?"

"I'm gonna ask Tony, the head of valet parking, if he can give me a ride," Kennin said.

"And what about school tomorrow morning?" Mariel asked.

"I don't know. Same as today, I guess."

They were on the strip now, and could see the Babylon up ahead.

"You could stay at my house," Mariel suddenly said.

This caught Kennin by surprise. He stared at her. "You think your parents would go for that?"

"They don't care," Mariel said. "You know the cabana outside by the pool?"

Kennin remembered it from the party where Cousin Raoul had pulled a knife to keep Kennin from tearing Ian's head off. Normally, he would have refused the offer. It would cause nothing but trouble. But if he went home tonight he faced three problems. Two of them—not having money for

the rent and not having a way to get to school tomorrow—
might not kill him. But the third—Jack—just might.

"That's a really nice offer," Kennin said. "Suppose I
accept. This isn't something you'd be telling anyone,
right?"

"Not if you don't want me to," Mariel said.

"And how would I get to your house tonight after work?"

"What time are you finished?" Mariel asked.

"Midnight."

Mariel smiled. "See you then."

13

After Mariel dropped Kennin at the parking garage, Tony came out of the valet office with a casino security guard in a gray uniform. Tony had a serious look on his face. "Mr. Mercado wants to see you."

"Why?" Kennin asked.

"You got me." Tony gestured to the guard. "Joe'll take you into the casino."

Kennin followed the security guard inside and past the public elevators to the small private one that required a key. They rode up to the penthouse in silence. The elevator stopped and the doors opened into a dark-wood-paneled office. Laney, an attractive blond woman wearing glasses, sat at a desk typing on a silver laptop computer. She smiled at him. "Please take a seat, Kennin. Mr. Mercado will be right with you."

Kennin sat down on a small couch. Hanging on the wall

opposite him was a brightly colored painting of Formula One Grand Prix cars careening around a curb in a splash of brilliant hues. Kennin had never seen a painting of racing cars before. He got up to take a closer look.

"You like it?" a voice asked.

Kennin turned to find Mike Mercado in the doorway. He was wearing blue slacks, a white shirt, a red tie, and blue suspenders.

"Yes," Kennin answered.

"It's by LeRoy Neiman," Mercado said. "Ever heard of him?"

Kennin shook his head.

Mercado smiled. "Well, come on in. You want anything?"

"I'm fine, thanks," Kennin said, and followed Mercado through the large dark wooden doors and into his office. Kennin had been in the office once before, but the size of it still amazed him. It was lined with dark red curtains and must have taken up at least half of the top floor of the casino building.

Mercado led Kennin to the easy chairs in the front of a huge flat-screen TV. On the other side of the room was a Ping-Pong table, and against the wall stood an enormous fish tank filled with colorful tropical fish. In the middle of the office was a sleek red and white motorcycle. On Kennin's last visit Mercado had told him it was a Ducati Desmosedici, the fastest production motorcycle in the world.

"Still haven't taken it for a test drive?" Kennin asked.

"No way," Mercado said. "I value life too highly. Especially mine." They sat down in the chairs. "How's the leg?"

"Better, thanks."

"Strange for a wheel to break off like that right at the beginning of a run, isn't it?" Mercado asked.

Kennin nodded.

"Of course, if that had happened on our new track instead of up in the mountains, there wouldn't have been nearly as much damage," Mercado said. "I doubt you'd have even been hurt."

Kennin knew that Mercado hadn't invited him there to remind him of the dangers of drifting on dark mountain roads.

"Derek tells me you're reluctant to get involved with our new project," the casino owner said. "Is it because of the crash?"

Not wanting to say one way or the other, Kennin shrugged. "The car's trashed."

"Anything else you can drive?" Mercado asked.

"Maybe," Kennin said, thinking of Shinchou's Corolla. "But the vehicle I'm thinking of needs a lot of work."

Mercado rubbed his chin thoughtfully. "Would five thousand be enough?"

Kennin blinked. For a moment he wondered if he'd heard the casino owner correctly. "Sorry, sir?"

"Five thousand dollars to get this other car running," Mercado repeated.

That time Kennin knew he'd heard him right. "Please don't take this the wrong way, sir, but why me?" he said. "I mean, I already know you got me out of a lot of trouble because of the crash. And now you want to give me all this money."

Mercado cocked his head curiously. "And you want to know what I want in return for my five thousand bucks? I want a good-looking kid with a charismatic personality who happens to be a great drifter to bring a lot of excitement to our new drift track. I think that's worth five grand, don't you?"

Kennin ran his fingers through his hair. "Like I said before, sir, it's a fantastic offer and I really appreciate it. I just need some time to think. A lot's happened lately."

Mike Mercado's eyebrows dipped, and Kennin could see that the casino owner was disappointed. "I'd think you would have had enough time by now. Derek tells me he spoke to you about the team weeks ago."

"I know, sir," Kennin said. "It's not easy to explain. I just need a little more time."

Mercado frowned and stood up. "All right, Kennin. You think about it and let me know."

Kennin got up, and Mercado walked him to the door.

"I guess a crash like that could shake you up, huh?" Mercado said as he held open the door.

"It can have that effect, sir," Kennin replied, and went out.

The security guard escorted Kennin out of the casino. Tony was standing outside the valet parking office with Tito when Kennin returned. Tito had his BMX and had just gotten there.

"Everything okay?" he asked.

"Yeah, no problem," said Kennin.

Tony appeared relieved, and for a moment Kennin wondered if he knew something Kennin didn't.

"Okay, go change into your uniform," Tony said. "We got some cars to wash."

"Tony said Mercado wanted to talk to you," Tito said in the locker room while they changed. "What's up?"

"He wanted to know why I haven't joined the team," said Kennin.

"He's not the only one," said Tito.

"I told him I'd let him know," Kennin said.

Tito stared at him in wonder. "You told Mike Mercado you'd let him know? Dude, I hope you know what you're doing."

Kennin hoped so too.

They were busy washing cars for most of the evening. Around eleven. Tony came out of the valet office. "Okay, guys, I'm heading out. Make sure everything's locked up when you leave, okay?"

"Sure."

Fifteen minutes later Tito's cell phone rang. "Yeah?

Hey, where ya been, Raoul? What? Crap! How would I know? I thought you were in the frickin' gardening business! Okay, okay, hold on for a second!"

Tito quickly turned to Kennin. "It's Raoul. He did it again. Boosted a car with LoJack. He figures he's two minutes ahead of the cops and he wants to know what to do."

"Have him bring it here," Kennin said.

"Are you crazy?" Tito gasped.

"Tell him to go up to the fifth level," Kennin said, "and make sure he parks between two cars."

Tito's jaw dropped. "I get it! With all the cars in this place, it'll take the cops forever to work their way up!"

Kennin pointed at the phone. "He's running out of time."

Tito pressed the phone to his ear. "Raoul? Bring the car to the Babylon. The parking garage. Go up to the fifth level and park between some cars."

Tito was just about to disconnect when Kennin thought of something else. "Ask him if he's wearing his driving gloves."

"Huh?" Tito scowled at him.

"Just do it," Kennin urged.

"You wearing gloves?" Tito asked into the phone. "No?"

"Okay, just tell him to get here fast," Kennin said.

A moment later Tito flipped the phone closed.

"Let's go," Kennin said as he tossed some chammies into a bucket and headed for the stairs.

"We're gonna wash the car?" Tito asked, confused.

"No, we're gonna wipe the prints. Your cousin's been in jail, remember? It's not enough to just ditch the car. We have to get rid of the evidence, too."

"We gotta run up five floors?" Tito asked.

"You know a better way to get up there?" Kennin asked back.

"Yeah, the elevator," Tito said.

"We're not allowed in the casino without permission," Kennin said. "Mr. Mercado wouldn't want to hear that his two car washers were in the elevators on their way upstairs to wipe a stolen car."

"Dude, can I ask you a question?" Tito huffed and panted as they climbed the stairs. "How do you know about all this stuff? Like wiping cars and crap. What were you back in Pasadena, a professional car thief?"

"We've still got three floors to go," Kennin answered. "Better save your breath."

The fifth floor was only half-filled with cars. There were plenty of open spaces for Raoul to stick the vehicle he'd stolen.

"I have to hand it to you, Kennin," Tito said as he caught his breath from climbing the stairs. "This is frickin' brilliant. LoJack may be good horizontally, but it don't work so good vertically. The cops are gonna have to go through four floors' worth of cars before they get here."

"Unless they decide to start at the top and work their way down," Kennin reminded him.

Tito's eyes bulged. "Oh, crap, that's right!"

They could hear the sound of screeching tires in the distance, gradually growing louder.

"So what happened to Cousin Raoul's gardening business?" Kennin asked.

Tito shrugged. "Guess it was too much work for not enough money. The last time I saw him, he complained that he was clearing eight hundred a week busting his hump in the sun all day. He said boosting cars he could make the same amount in a couple of hours."

The screech of skidding tires and the wail of police sirens were growing louder.

"Crime pays well until you get caught," Kennin said.

"You speaking from experience?" Tito asked.

There was a loud skidding squeal below them as a car raced into the parking garage. They listened to the engine rev as it climbed the ramps toward the top level. Kennin reached into the bucket and tossed Tito a chammie. "You take the outside. Door handles, window frames, trunk, anything you think Raoul might have touched. I'll get the inside."

Tito started to look excited. "What do you think it'll be, huh? Another GTO? Or a 'vette? Maybe a Benz or a Beemer?"

From the sound of the exhaust, Kennin already knew it was Japanese and a four-cylinder. A second later a red Camry swung around the corner and sped up toward them.

"A Camry?" Tito sounded disgusted.

As soon as Kennin saw the car, he knew Raoul was working for a professional ring. Tito's cousin wasn't out for a joyride this time. Camrys were stolen for one reason: to sell to chop shops, where they could be dismantled and the parts sold for considerably more than the car was worth.

Kennin waved at Raoul to park between a Benz and a Volvo. Tito's cousin screeched the car to a stop and jumped out. Raoul was an older guy with short-cropped brown hair. His eyebrows, ears, and lip were pierced, and both arms were almost entirely covered with dark sleeves of tattoos. "Guys, I don't know how to thank you!"

The sound of more squealing tires came from below as the cops arrived.

"Figure it out someplace else," Kennin said. "Right now, just get the hell out of here."

Raoul bolted for the exit. Meanwhile, things had grown quiet below. Kennin had a feeling the cops were hatching a plan.

"Raoul!" Kennin hissed just as Tito's cousin reached the door to the stairs. "Don't take the stairs! Take the elevator down to the casino. Go play blackjack for a couple of hours."

"Gotcha." Raoul disappeared through the exit. Tito

started wiping down the outside of the car. Kennin got in and wiped the steering wheel, the shifter, and anything else Raoul might have touched.

Suddenly Tito straightened up. He grabbed the car door and pulled it open. "I hear voices," he whispered. "They're close!"

"Time to bounce," Kennin whispered back, getting out of the Camry and wiping away any trail of prints he might have left in the process.

"Come on!" Tito hissed nervously.

Kennin pressed a finger against his lips, and they headed for the doorway that led to the stairs. Kennin quietly opened the door, but stopped.

"What's wrong?" Tito whispered.

"Footsteps coming up the stairs." Kennin slowly let the door close again.

Tito quickly looked around and got jumpy. "What're we gonna do?" he gasped. "We can't go down and we can't stay here or we'll get caught."

"This way," Kennin whispered, and started to jog up the ramp.

"But that just leads to the top level," Tito said. "If the cops find the car and not the driver, they're gonna think he went up here."

"You got a better idea?"

"Crap!" Tito muttered.

They ran up to the roof level. The December night air

was cold. Except for half a dozen cars, the top level was empty. Just concrete and yellow lined spaces. Under the vast starlit sky above, they quickly looked around for a place to hide. "There!" Tito pointed at the square concrete elevator housing.

"No!" Kennin said. "That's exactly where they'd expect us to hide."

"Then where?" Tito asked.

Kennin looked around and pointed.

Tito frowned. "There's nothing but a wall."

Kennin knew that. He also knew that the cops were going to be there in less than a minute.

They reached the wall and Kennin looked over the side. Except for a row of stubby cell phone antennas bolted to the outside wall about two feet below the ledge, it was six stories straight down to the street.

"Come on," Kennin said, and started to shimmy over the ledge.

Tito froze. "Are you insane?"

"You want to get nailed?" Kennin asked.

Tito didn't answer. With wide eyes he watched as Kennin slid over the ledge and carefully lowered himself onto a cell phone antenna, straddling it as if it was a tree branch. When it didn't break off under Kennin's weight, Tito decided to give it a try, carefully inching over the ledge and letting himself down onto the antenna next to Kennin's.

Now they were both perched six stories up on the outside

wall of the parking garage, straddling cell phone antennas, their feet hanging in the air. Cars passed on the street below and couples strolled along the sidewalk. One slip and it was six stories straight down. Tito held the cell phone antenna so tightly his knuckles turned white.

"I don't like this," he hissed through clenched teeth.

"Relax," Kennin whispered back. More cars passed on the streets below, and some kind of bird glided past above, lit from beneath by the thousands of watts of neon and incandescent lights.

"Relax? Are you out of your frickin' mind?" Tito raised his voice. "How am I supposed to relax?"

"Shut it!" Kennin hissed. "Enjoy the view."

"The things I frickin' let you talk me into," Tito muttered.

"Don't thank me, thank Cousin Raoul."

"If I knew I was gonna wind up risking my life for that idiot," Tito said, "I would have let the cops get him."

Suspended on the outside wall, Kennin couldn't hear what was happening with the cops. It was impossible to even know if they'd gotten up to the roof level yet. He heard a loud roar approaching and looked up as a jet passed overhead, the dark underside appearing a lot closer than it would have at street level.

"How long we gonna have to stay here?" Tito whispered after the jet passed.

"Till they leave," Kennin whispered back.

"How're we gonna know when that is?" Tito asked.

Just then a deep male voice came from the other side of the wall: "Let's try up here."

Tito's eyes went wide. He and Kennin could hear footsteps on the roof level.

"Look on top of the elevator," someone said.

"And under those cars, too."

On the other side of the wall, Tito and Kennin stared at each other for a while. Then Kennin tilted his head back till it touched the wall, and closed his eyes. A slight breeze fluttered his hair, and he felt a shiver. The night air was cold and they weren't wearing jackets. There was nothing to do but "hang around" and wait.

They heard footsteps and grunts as cops got down on their knees and looked under cars. Now and then the beam of a flashlight would swing over the ledge above them. Then Kennin heard a loud scrape just a few feet away on the other side of the wall, and a voice said, "I'm going to look over here."

15

Perched on the cell phone antenna, Kennin stared at Tito. The kid's eyes were bugging out of his head, and his mouth hung open, his lower lip quivering. Kennin quickly shook his head. A flashlight beam swung right over them.

Kennin heard heavy breathing. Tito's mouth was agape and he was staring straight down. The kid was freaking. Kennin let go of the antenna with one hand and reached over, placing it on Tito's shoulder to steady him. Tito quickly swiveled his head toward Kennin. His face was pale and speckled with sweat.

Kennin mouthed the words, "Don't look down." Tito took a deep breath and nodded.

A minute later a voice above them said, "No sign of anyone."

"He must've gone into the casino," said someone else. "Maybe took the elevator down."

"If he's in the casino, at least we know the perp must be eighteen."

"Or he looks eighteen."

Footsteps began to move away. Perhaps twenty seconds passed, and then Tito started to stretch up as if to look over the edge. Once again Kennin grabbed him by the shoulder and shook his head. It was too soon. A favorite trick of the cops was to pretend to leave and then see who popped up.

So they stayed where they were. Kennin heard chattering teeth. They were Tito's. At least once a minute the guy would whisper, "Now?" and Kennin would shake his head. The longer they waited the better. Finally, when even Kennin couldn't stand waiting anymore, they climbed back over the ledge.

The roof level was empty. The cops were gone. Tito and Kennin walked across the lot and then down the ramps back to the first floor. Tito dragged his feet and looked drained.

"I can't take this," he moaned through chattering teeth. "You gotta have nerves of steel for this stuff. I've got nerves of bubblegum."

"Tell Cousin Raoul not to steal any more cars," Kennin suggested.

"Right," Tito scoffed. "I might as well tell my dog to stop licking his nuts. Ain't gonna happen, *amigo*."

They got back down to the valet office. Tito looked up at the clock. "Five of twelve, dude. Almost closing time. How're you gonna get home?"

The words had hardly left his lips when Mariel pulled up in the red Lexus. Kennin watched Tito's jaw drop.

"No way!" he gasped under his breath.

"It's not what it seems," Kennin said in a low voice.

"Oh, sure," Tito smirked. "It's midnight and the hottest girl in school is picking you up and it's not what it seems. Mariel just happened to be passing by here exactly at closing time and just happened to stop in because somehow she miraculously knew that you'd need a ride home."

Kennin couldn't help but be amused. He wondered how Tito would react if he knew Mariel wasn't there to take him to his place, but to hers.

"Catch you tomorrow," Kennin said.

"Yeah, sure," Tito said. "In the meantime, I hope you get some sleep tonight."

"It's not like that," Kennin said.

"Anything you say," Tito grumbled, and went to get his BMX bike.

Kennin got into the Lexus. It was fragrant with perfume. "Thanks for picking me up."

"My pleasure," Mariel said with a smile, and started to drive. "So how was work?"

"The same as always," Kennin replied with a shrug.

"What's your job?" she asked as they rode through the dark.

"Washing cars."

"Much of a future in that?" she asked.

"Maybe if you're the guy who owns the car wash," Kennin said.

"Think you'll be that guy someday?" Mariel asked.

"Not a clue. How about you?"

"I'll wait till college to decide," Mariel said. "Sometimes I think about acting."

Appropriate choice, Kennin thought.

They entered Mariel's neighborhood, passing large houses with red or blue tile roofs and broad green lawns. It was after midnight, and most of the windows were dark. The streets were lined with palm trees, and the driveways had shiny new cars parked in them. Kennin lowered the passenger window to smell the sweet, moist air.

Mariel pulled the Lexus into the driveway, next to a big Mercedes sedan. Like the other houses on the street, the windows in her parents' house were dark.

"Close the door quietly," she whispered as they got out of the Lexus. In the dark driveway she took his hand and led him around the side of the house.

"You're not going to tell your parents I'm staying here?" Kennin whispered.

"I will," Mariel whispered back. "When the time is right."

They went around to the back of the house. Unlike the last time Kennin had been here, the pool was dark. The only sound was the whirring of the filtration system. Still holding his hand tightly in hers, Mariel led him to the cabana. She quietly turned the door knob, opened the door, and led him inside.

Kennin expected her to flick on the lights and show him around. Instead, Mariel turned to him in the dark and slid her hands around his waist, pulling him closer until their bodies pressed against each other.

16

Mariel drove him to school the next morning, but Kennin insisted she drop him off a couple of blocks away so that he could walk. The last thing he needed was rumors starting because people saw him getting out of her car. In the afternoon he walked a few blocks and then she picked him up and drove him the rest of the way to work.

But the third afternoon when Kennin left school, he saw a familiar-looking dark green unmarked cop car parked at the curb. Inside sat Detective Neilson. Kennin caught the detective's eye and nodded. Then he motioned with his head down the block. Neilson nodded back and drove slowly to the corner.

Kennin turned the corner. Then, away from the rest of the kids, he leaned into the window of the detective's car. "What's the word?"

Neilson jerked his head over to the passenger side. "Get in."

"We going somewhere?"

"Just get in," Neilson growled. He was not in a good mood, and it was best to do what he said. Kennin got into the car. Neilson was wearing an ugly brown overcoat that did not go well with his new look. On the sidewalk a few kids from school passed. One or two looked into the car and saw Kennin.

"Think you could drive, so these kids don't see me?" Kennin asked.

Neilson put the car into gear and pulled away from the curb. "How's your sister?"

"You came all the way here to ask me that?" Kennin asked.

"Hey," Neilson snapped sharply. "Watch your mouth."

Kennin stared out the window.

"Still working over at the Babylon parking garage?" the detective asked.

"That's right."

"Know anything about a stolen Camry that wound up on the fifth floor the other night?"

Kennin shook his head.

"Funny thing is, the lab guys went over it and the entire car was wiped clean," Neilson said. "No prints at all. Not even the owner's. Makes you wonder how the car even got there."

"Maybe the owner wore gloves," Kennin said.

"Yeah, I thought of that too," Neilson said. "So I asked Mrs. Johnson. She's the car's owner. And guess what? She's never worn gloves while driving in her life. She's afraid the wheel will slip."

"Guess she doesn't know about racing gloves," Kennin said.

"Guess not," said Neilson. "So back to my original question. How do you think the car got wiped clean?"

"You said it was stolen," Kennin asked. "So maybe the thief wiped it clean."

"Well, _somebody_ wiped it clean, that's for sure," Neilson said. "And that's the strange thing, because while the lab guys couldn't find any prints, they did find residue on the car of some special pH-balanced soaps with lubricants."

Kennin scowled and raised his palms upward questioningly. As if to say, _So?_

"So it turns out Mrs. Johnson never uses that stuff," Neilson said.

"She washes the car herself?" Kennin asked.

"No, she usually goes to the Five Hands Car Wash," Neilson said. "Strange thing is, they don't use those kinds of soaps either. But guess who does?"

The answer was obvious. "Mr. Mercado has us use them on his cars," Kennin answered.

Neilson nodded. "You and Tito Rivera, right?"

"Yes, sir."

"So tell me, Kennin, how in the world do you think Mrs. Johnson's car got wiped down with the same rags—"

"We don't use rags," Kennin interrupted. "We use chammies. Sheepskin."

Neilson raised an eyebrow. "Very fancy. So how did her car get wiped down with Mr. Mercado's chammies?"

Kennin shrugged.

"Where are the chammies usually kept, Kennin?" the detective asked.

"In a closet next to the valet parking office," Kennin said.

"Is the closet usually locked?"

Kennin shook his head.

Neilson sighed. "And next you're going to tell me you have no idea how chammies in a closet on the first floor were used to wipe a stolen Camry on the fifth floor. Like I'm supposed to believe that every car thief in Las Vegas knows the chammies are there. And that with three police cruisers chasing him, this particular car thief had the wherewithal to stop on the first floor and pick up a few chammies. Then drive up to the fifth floor and carefully wipe down both the inside and the outside of the car. And then stroll away."

"If you say so," Kennin replied.

"And that leads to my next question," Neilson said. "Just how do you think the chammies that were used on the fifth floor got back down to the closet on the first floor?"

"Maybe they didn't," Kennin said.

"You missing any chammies?" the detective asked.

"I wouldn't know."

"Would Tito Rivera know?"

"Why don't you ask him?"

Neilson drummed his fingers on the steering wheel and was quiet for a moment. "You're a pretty cool character, Kennin. Especially for a sixteen-year-old. But that in itself speaks volumes, know what I mean? It tells me you've been here before. It tells me you've had a lot of experience dealing with cops."

Kennin stared down at an empty can of Diet Mountain Dew on the floor of the car. "Listen, Detective Neilson, I know you're only doing your job, so here's the real deal. I don't steal cars anymore, okay? Maybe I did some dumb stuff back in California, but that was a long time ago in a galaxy far away. I'm finished with that now."

"You got any outstanding warrants?" Neilson asked.

Kennin shook his head. "The charges were adjudicated. Youthful offender. The records are sealed."

Neilson raised a blond eyebrow. "You telling me you learned your lesson?"

"You could say that," Kennin said. "You could say that I don't want to end up like my father. You could say that mostly, I'd just like to be left alone."

"But you still haven't told me everything you know about the Camry," Neilson said. "Or about the GTO."

"You know that saying about being caught between a rock and a hard place?" Kennin asked.

"Sometimes you have to take sides," said Neilson.

"Against my family and friends?"

"People do it all the time," Neilson said.

Kennin didn't bother to reply. He just gazed out the window.

"So, seriously, what is going on with your sister?" Neilson asked.

"What do you care?" Kennin asked.

"You don't trust anyone, do you?" Neilson said.

Kennin tried to think about who he could really trust. Only two people came to mind: his sister, as long as she wasn't totally strung out. And Angelita.

"She's okay," Kennin said.

"My guys tell me they haven't seen her around," Neilson said.

"That's right," said Kennin.

"I hear certain people are kind of upset," Neilson said. "They've been looking for her."

Kennin placed his shoe on the empty Mountain Dew can and slowly began to crush it.

"I could help make sure they don't find her," Neilson offered. "But I'd need something in return."

Kennin nodded. The detective steered the car over to the curb and stopped. "You can go. Just think about what I said."

Kennin got out. He was a few blocks from school and assumed he would have to walk back to meet Mariel. So he was surprised when she pulled up to the curb in front of him. He opened the door and got in.

"You followed us?" he asked.

"I saw you get in the car," Mariel replied as she pulled away from the curb. "So that was a detective, right?"

"How'd you know?" Kennin asked.

This time it was Mariel's turn to shrug mysteriously.

17

The next morning, after first-period geometry class, Kennin stepped out into the hall and almost bumped into Tito and Angelita.

"What are you doing here?" Tito asked him.

"In school?" Kennin replied. "They tell me it's required by law."

Angelita smiled.

"But this early?" Tito said. "The bus strike's still on. Don't tell me Mariel's driving over to your place every morning and giving you a ride."

The smile disappeared from Angelita's face. Kennin wondered why she and Tito were together. They rarely spent time with each other in school.

Luckily, Tito had more pressing news. "You hear about Chris? He's on the Babylon team. Driftdog Dave made it too. Everyone wants to know when you're gonna try out."

Kennin's eyes darted back and forth between Angelita and Tito. "How many times are you gonna ask me that?"

"Things have changed," Tito said. "The 'no car' excuse doesn't wash anymore." He glanced at his sister.

"I talked to Shinchou," Angelita said.

Kennin stared at Tito, who'd promised not to tell anyone where Shinchou was.

"Look, I told my sister, okay?" Tito dropped his voice. "You know you can trust her. And I did it for your sake, so chill already."

Kennin felt his fists tighten. He was seriously pissed, but there was little he could say in front of Angelita.

"How is she?" he asked Tito's sister. Kennin had been afraid to go see his sister himself. He was worried that Jack, or someone who worked for Jack, would follow him.

"She looked okay," Angelita said. "I mean, I guess what she's doing is pretty stressful, but she seemed glad she was doing it."

"Did she say anything?" Kennin asked.

"Just that it was really hard. I guess Sista Bertha insists you quit everything at once. Shinchou wasn't sure which she missed more, the meth or the cigarettes."

"She's not angry at me, is she?" Kennin asked.

"I got the sense she thinks you're a good brother." Angelita smiled, obviously happy with what she was about to tell him. "Besides, if she was angry at you, would she say it was okay to use her car?"

"What does she have to lose?" Tito asked eagerly. "All we're gonna do is fix the thing up for her."

"You really think a Corolla has much of a chance against turbocharged 240 SXs and RX-7s?" Kennin asked. But the words had barely left his lips when he remembered the five grand Mike Mercado was willing to invest.

"It might in the right hands," Angelita said. "And on the right track."

"Come on, Kennin, no more messing around," Tito said. "You'll do it, won't you?"

Kennin could see the flicker of hope in Angelita's eyes. "I don't get it," he said. "I thought you were all about going to California."

Angelita lowered her eyes, then raised them again. "I am," she said. "But I'd like to do this before I go."

After school, as usual, Mariel met Kennin a few blocks from school to give him a ride to work.

"Chris is on the team," Kennin said.

Mariel shrugged. "He's good at getting what he wants."

Interesting comment, Kennin thought, since the same could be said about her.

Mariel glanced sideways at him. "I'm keeping my promise and not asking about you and the team."

"Looks like I'm gonna have to decide pretty soon," Kennin said.

"I don't understand what the problem is," Mariel said. "You love drifting, don't you?"

"It's more complicated than that," Kennin said.

"No one made you run in the tsuisos," Mariel said.

There was no point in explaining that running tsuisos on mountain roads was different from sliding around cones on a track. Or that as soon as you combined the words "organized" and "drifting," the BS factor increased a hundredfold.

Mariel dropped him off at the parking garage. As Kennin got out of the car, Tito came down the sidewalk on his BMX bike.

"What is she? Your personal chauffeur?" he asked after Mariel drove away.

"You should be happy," Kennin said. "I'm leaving your sister alone, just like you want."

Before Tito could reply, a big black Hummer pulled into the garage. Derek rolled down the window and looked out at Kennin. "You're a hard guy to find."

"Looks like you found me," Kennin said.

Derek pushed open the Hummer's door and stepped down. Without a word, Tony came out of the valet office and parked the car.

"Let's take a walk," Derek said.

"What about me?" Tito asked.

"You stay," Derek said. It was obvious that he was in a

bad mood. He and Kennin left the garage and started to stroll down the sidewalk, past the tourists and out-of-town gamblers who would soon be going home broke.

"Not living in the trailer park anymore?" Derek asked.

"What can I do for you, Mr. Jamison?" Kennin cut to the chase.

"It's time to stop screwing around, kid," Derek said. "Mr. Mercado made you a very nice offer, and it's time you accepted it."

"I told Mr. Mercado that I'd think about it," Kennin replied.

"Let me explain something to you, kid," Derek said. "People don't tell Mr. Mercado they'll think about things, okay? You do what he says or you suffer the consequences. Now, he wants a rivalry between you and Chris Craven, okay? Nobody wants to watch the Yankees play the Colorado Rockies, but when the Yankees play the Red Sox, you can't find a seat. Michigan versus Ohio State, Auburn versus Alabama, USC versus UCLA. That's what brings people out. Now, I've known Mike Mercado a long time and I've never seen him be this generous before. That's not a five grand *loan* he's talking about. It's a frickin' gift. No one thumbs his nose at a gift from Mike Mercado."

"I guess he could break my other leg," Kennin said. "Or is it time for that shallow grave in the desert?"

Derek let out a big sigh. "All right, kid, let me explain it to you in a different way. Car washers are a dime a dozen.

Mr. Mercado don't need you to wash cars. He can find a hundred other kids to do that. And he definitely don't need kids who borrow his clients' BMWs for a few hours without permission. So there's your choice, either Mr. Mercado thinks of you as a drifter on his team, or as a car washer who tends to borrow cars that ain't his."

Kennin didn't like to be threatened. He didn't see the point in it.

"You know, Mr. Jamison," he said. "You're right that car washers are a dime a dozen, but the flip side of that is that there are a hundred other jobs around here that pay just as badly. So if I lose this one, chances are pretty good I'll find another one."

Like an experienced boxer, Derek came right back with another punch. "You're tough, and I admire that in you, but you haven't learned to recognize when the cards are stacked against you, okay? And this is one of those times. So which card would you like me to play next? How about the 'I know where your sister is' card? And here's another one. I know there's a slimeball pimp and drug dealer who's looking real hard for her. How's that card sound?"

Kennin stopped walking and gave Derek an astonished look.

"Come on, kid, you're smarter than that," Derek said. "You must've figured out by now that you can't keep a secret in this town."

"Tito told you?" Kennin asked.

Derek shook his head.

"Then how?"

Derek gave him a steady look and said nothing.

"If you know, maybe a lot of people know," Kennin said. "Maybe it's not a secret anymore. So my doing anything for you won't help anyway."

Derek gave Kennin a weary look. "I guess there's one way to find out. You willing to give it a try?"

Kennin didn't have to think about it for long. "If I take Mr. Mercado's five thousand and build a drift car, can you swear that no one else will find out where my sister is?"

"I can swear that they won't find out from me," Derek said.

Kennin knew he'd been backed into a corner. "Okay," he said. "But so help me, if anything happens to my sister, I am coming after you."

Derek grinned. "I admire your spunk, kid." He reached into his jacket pocket and pulled out an envelope. "This is for the car and nothing else, understand? I find out a penny of this money went anywhere else, the deal's off, and I won't be able to vouch for what happens to your sister, understand?"

Kennin nodded and took the envelope. He turned around and started back toward the Babylon. By the time he got there, he had an idea.

"So what was that about?" Tito asked in the locker room a few minutes later while he and Kennin changed into their uniforms.

"I'll tell you when the time is right," Kennin said. "Cousin Raoul still have his van?"

"I guess, why?" Tito asked.

"See if he can meet us after school tomorrow." It was their day off from work.

"What's the deal?" Tito asked.

"I need him to return a favor."

Tito called his cousin, who said he'd be glad to meet them.

"Tell him to bring about a dozen long screws," Kennin said before Tito closed the flip phone. "Wood screws, not machine screws."

Tito made a face. "Why?"

"Just do it."

18

The next day after school, Raoul's white van was parked in front of the building.

"What am I gonna do with my bike?" Tito asked when he and Kennin came out of the front doors.

"Put it in the back," Kennin said. While Tito unlocked the BMX, Kennin went over and said hello to Raoul.

"Kennin, my man." Raoul grabbed his hand.

"Stayin' out of trouble?" Kennin kidded him.

"Tryin', *amigo*, tryin'. So what can I do for you today?"

"I'll tell you on the way," Kennin said. "Let's get Tito's bike in the back."

Raoul pulled open the back doors. He still had the lawnmower back there, and the van smelled like dead grass. They picked up the BMX and put it inside, and then the three of them got into the bench seat in front. A plastic bag with screws lay on the dashboard.

"Where to?" Raoul asked.

"Know where the Sierra Ne-Vue trailer park is?" Kennin asked.

"I think so." Raoul started to drive.

"Why are we going there?" Tito asked.

"Gotta pick up a car."

"Your sister's?" Tito guessed.

"Right."

"So what do you need the screws for?" Tito asked.

"You'll see," said Kennin.

A little while later they drove past the dead palm trees at the entrance to the trailer park.

"Where we going?" Raoul asked.

"Straight to the end," Kennin said. As they passed his trailer, he saw the black Escalade parked outside. He wasn't surprised that Jack had posted a full-time guard there to wait for Shinchou to come home.

"Okay, stop," Kennin said.

Raoul stopped the van, and Kennin pointed through the window. "See that Escalade? We have to make it go away. Only there's a guy inside it who doesn't want to go away."

"Oh, crap," Tito groaned. "Here we go again."

"So what's the plan?" Raoul asked.

Kennin told them.

"No! No way!" Tito protested when Kennin was finished. "No frickin' way."

Kennin just gazed steadily at him, waiting for Tito to realize that he was going to do it.

"I know what you're thinking and I don't care," Tito said. "Go ahead and tell my sister anything you want."

"Tell her what?" Raoul asked.

"Well, you see, Raoul," Kennin began. "You know that 240 SX that Angelita spent so much time and money building?"

"All right!" Tito blurted. "All right, I'll do it. But this is it. I swear. This is the end. Never again."

"Gotcha," Kennin said with a wink, then turned to Raoul. "You know what to do?"

Tito's cousin nodded.

"Okay," Kennin said. "See you guys later." He grabbed the bag of screws and got out of the truck.

Staying behind trailers, Kennin managed to work his way back to his own while keeping out of sight of the Escalade. As he did, he kept an eye on Raoul's van and watched as Tito and his cousin quietly opened the back doors and took out the BMX bike. A few moments later the white van left the trailer park.

Kennin had reached the corner of his trailer. Now came the tricky part. He had to get behind the Escalade without being seen. If Tiny happened to glance into the rearview mirror while Kennin was making his dash, he'd be toast. Clutching the bag of screws in his hand, Kennin took a deep breath, and then tiptoed as quickly and quietly as he could.

A moment later he was crouching behind the Escalade, trying to catch his breath. He didn't hear or sense any movement from inside the SUV.

He knelt down and started to wedge the screws, pointed end up, against the rear tires so that when the Escalade reversed, the screws would be driven straight through the tread and into the steel bands beneath. When he finished, he once again scampered around the corner of the trailer.

It was time for Tito to do his thing. Kennin waved, and Tito grabbed the handlebars of the bike and walked it out into the open about fifty feet behind the Escalade. He put down the kickstand, picked up a chunk of broken asphalt, and threw it at the back of the Escalade.

The asphalt missed. Tito gave Kennin a helpless look. Kennin gestured for the kid to try again. Tito picked up another chunk and hurled it.

Clank! The asphalt hit the back of the SUV.

Tito gave Kennin a nervous look. Kennin gestured for Tito to throw another one. Tito did it.

Clank!

This time the door of the Escalade opened and Tiny got out. "You throwin' rocks?" the big goon yelled at Tito.

Tito nervously glanced at Kennin, who quickly shook his head and backed out of sight. They couldn't let Tiny suspect that anyone else was involved.

"I hate SUVs!" Tito yelled and picked up another chunk of asphalt and threw it.

The asphalt missed.

"Are you crazy?" Tiny shouted.

"They use too much gas and cause global pollution warming!" Tito yelled and threw another chunk of asphalt.

Clank!

Tiny quickly started to climb back into the Escalade. That was Tito's cue to get on the bike and bounce.

19

Vroom! The SUV roared and started to back up. Kennin pictured the rear wheels rolling over the upturned screws. He heard a sound like a loud gasp but was certain that Tiny inside didn't hear it. The goon was already wheeling the Escalade around and following Tito on his BMX bike toward the exit.

Kennin didn't think the Escalade would get very far before it was riding on its rims. And it didn't matter anyway, because Raoul was waiting half a block away to throw the bike in the back of the van and get Tito out of there.

Still, Kennin knew he didn't have much time. He hurried into the trailer, grabbed some clothes and his sister's car keys, came back out, and jumped into the Corolla. A few moments later, as he drove his sister's car out of the trailer park, he spied the Escalade on the side of the road. Both rear tires were flat. Tiny was standing beside the car, gesturing excitedly and speaking into a cell phone. Kennin was pretty sure he never even saw Shinchou's Corolla pass.

Kennin drove the Corolla to Rivera's Service Center. Raoul's van was parked on the street outside. Angelita, Tito, and Raoul were waiting by the garage door. Angelita was wearing coveralls, her black hair pulled back in a ponytail and her head covered with a red bandanna.

"It went okay, right?" Tito said excitedly as Kennin drove the car into the garage.

"Yup," Kennin replied. "Thanks, guys."

"Are you kidding?" Tito exclaimed. "I was just telling Angie how cool it was!" He turned to his sister. "You wouldn't believe the size of that guy! He must've weighed four hundred pounds! The second he starts climbing into the Escalade, I'm on the BMX and out of there riding as fast as I can! The Escalade comes flying out behind me, but as soon as it makes a left onto the road I start to hear all this racket. Like floppy flat tires getting torn up by the rims. I look behind me and the Escalade's stopped on the shoulder. Meanwhile, Raoul's waiting with the back doors of the van open and that wooden ramp thing for the lawnmower down, so I ride right up into the van like frickin' *Triple X*! Raoul slams the back doors, jumps in the driver's seat, and we're out of there."

It was obvious that Tito was totally pumped by the experience. "So now what?" he asked excitedly.

"Now we take a look at what we've got," Kennin said, gesturing toward the dirty yellow Corolla.

The excitement slowly drained from Tito's face. "Oh, man, I'm too stoked for that. I'm gonna go play GT4. I'll see you guys later."

"Thanks again," Kennin said as Tito left.

"Guess I'll split too," Raoul said.

"Hey, man, I can't thank you enough." Kennin offered him his hand.

"You kidding me?" Raoul replied. "It's me who should be thanking you, man. You've saved my butt twice."

"Stay out of trouble," Kennin said with a wave.

"I hear ya," Raoul said, then got into the van and left.

Kennin and Angelita were alone in the garage.

"So this is it," she said with a smile, running a finger along the Corolla's dirty fender and leaving a streak.

"Not much to look at," Kennin said.

"Not yet," Angelita replied, sticking her head into the passenger window. "Gotta start with a four-point harness." She opened the door and looked under the seat. "Seat bolts look okay." She stepped back and studied the car. "We'll have to find some extra wheels and a lot of tires."

Kennin couldn't help admiring the way she thought about the car. No BS. No stupid exterior mods. Just plain nuts and bolts. When she lifted the hood he came around and joined her. The engine was caked with black soot.

"It needs a better battery tie-down," Angelita said.

"What about the engine?" Kennin asked.

She shrugged. "I'll tune it the best I can."

"Be nice if you could drop that supercharged 4agze in," Kennin said.

"Be nice if I could do a lot of things." Angelita leaned her weight onto the fender and rocked the car. "Coilovers, new brakes, an ACT clutch."

"Don't forget," Kennin said, "we're talking tandem drifting."

Angelita's eyes widened slightly, then she shook her head and frowned. "I forgot. That's a whole different story. You need a six-point cage, buckets, and a harness. Plus a Nomex suit, shoes, head sock, helmet."

"What do you think it would cost?" Kennin asked.

Angelita's shoulders slumped. "What does it matter? You don't have that kind of money."

Kennin took out the white envelope Derek had given him and handed it to her.

"What's this?" Angelita asked uncertainly.

"Open it."

She opened the envelope just enough to peek inside, then quickly shut it. "Where did you get this?"

"Can't tell you," Kennin said.

Angelita held out the envelope. "Take it back. I don't want it."

"There's nothing wrong with it," Kennin said.

"Then where did it come from?" Angelita demanded.

"I'm sworn to secrecy," Kennin said. "But you can believe me, it's legitimate."

Angelita looked into the envelope again. "Since when are dirty, nonsequential twenty-dollar bills legitimate?"

"It's pocket change to the guy who gave it to me." As soon as the words left his lips, Kennin knew he'd said too much.

"What guy, Kennin?" Angelita asked.

Kennin stared at the floor. He knew what was coming.

"Kennin?" Angelita said again.

He shook his head. Angelita tossed the envelope onto the seat of the Corolla, then crossed her arms and leaned against the tool chest. "You can go now. I don't want that money, and I'm not touching that car."

Kennin realized he had no choice but to tell her. "You know who Mike Mercado is?"

"The owner of the Babylon?" Angelita said.

"He thinks that he needs me to drive against Chris to make it exciting and bring in a crowd."

"You didn't have to take it," Angelita said.

"I did," Kennin said. "There are other people who want me to drive. If I don't, they're liable to tell Jack where my sister is."

Angelita's forehead wrinkled. She gazed at the Corolla and then back at Kennin. "How much is in that envelope?"

"Four thousand," Kennin said. "Think it's enough?"

"Maybe," Angelita said. "But since we're laying our

cards on the table, there's something else. Tito tells me Mariel has become your private chauffeur."

"The buses are on strike," Kennin said.

"How generous of her," said Angelita. "What does Chris think?"

"She says she doesn't care," Kennin said. "But I've noticed she goes out of her way to try to make sure he doesn't know."

Angelita bit her lip and furrowed her brow. Kennin wondered if she was struggling with something. "Can I ask you something personal?" she said.

"Okay."

"Does . . . does Mariel do anything else besides drive you?" Angelita asked, then quickly added, "You can tell me if it's none of my business."

Kennin knew it had taken a lot for her to ask that question. Not only was she extra sensitive about not butting into other people's business, but it showed that she obviously still cared about him.

Kennin took a deep breath. He didn't want to lie to her, but there was no way she'd understand that sometimes when things were going badly and the temptations were too great, a guy might do something he'd later regret. "No, she doesn't do anything but drive."

20

 work on the Corolla every day after school. Kennin came by as often as he could to help and give her moral support. Angelita suspected that Mariel was dropping him off a block away, but she tried not to think too much about it. If that foolish girl wanted to drive Kennin around, that was her problem, not Angelita's.

She used the four thousand dollars wisely. Not a penny went toward unnecessary exterior mods. Except for a wash, the car's body looked no different from before.

At work both Derek and Mercado made a special point of telling Kennin they were pleased that he'd decided to drive. At the same time, billboards around town began advertising DriftVegas and word went out on drifting Web sites all over the West, inviting drivers to try out.

At school Chris wore a bright red and black racing jacket with his name embroidered on the front and "Babylon Drift

Team" scripted on the back. The arms of the jacket were adorned with patches from Cooper Tire, ACT clutches, Western Automotive, CIT Racing, and others. Heads turned wherever he went.

"It's like he's a frickin' movie star," Tito said at lunch the day of the DriftVegas event. When Chris and his posse entered the lunchroom, kids at other tables stopped what they were doing and stared at him. Kennin dabbed a French fry in ketchup and savored it, thankful that it wasn't a Tater Tot day.

"The guy's got sponsors up the wazoo!" Tito looked to see how Kennin was reacting, but his friend's expression didn't change.

"Dude, I think we missed the boat on that," Tito said. "By the way, you know, Angie didn't come to school today."

Kennin looked up at him, puzzled.

"She said there was still too much to do on the car," Tito explained. "Congratulations, dude, I can't remember a single time my sister ever ditched school. This is some kind of record."

Kennin nodded. Suddenly Tito let out a laugh. "Ha! There's Ian! And he's got a sponsor too!"

Kennin looked up. Ian entered the cafeteria wearing a red and white jacket that he'd clearly purchased on his own. Instead of Babylon Drift Team, scripted on the back of his jacket was "Monte's Fried Chicken."

Kennin ate another fry. He had to admit that fried chicken sounded pretty good.

Chris was sitting at the regular gearhead table, but Ian spotted Kennin and Tito and headed in their direction with some other guys.

"Uh-oh," Tito mumbled under his breath.

"Well, well, well." Ian stopped near their table. "If it isn't Fujiwara Takumi and his little AE86 Trueno."

Kennin gazed up at him. Ian had a contemptuous smirk on his face. "I hear you found a Corolla somewhere. You're not really serious, are you? I mean, taking that under-powered toy up against some world-class beaters?"

"What's with the Santa Claus suit?" Kennin asked. Some of the guys with Ian grinned.

"I'll be qualifying at DriftVegas tonight," Ian shot back. "Surprised? Or do you still think I can't drift?"

"He doesn't *think* you can't drift," Tito shot back. "He *knows* you can't drift, Mr. Fried Chicken."

Guys chuckled. Ian's face darkened and he balled his hands into fists. For a second it looked like he was going to launch himself at Tito, but Kennin got up and stood between them. "You got anything to prove, prove it tonight on the track."

It was one of those days when the seconds felt like minutes and the minutes felt like hours. As much as Kennin hated the idea of an organized drifting event on a track, he couldn't wait to get into the Corolla and see what it could do. When school ended, Tito was waiting for him at his locker.

"Psyched?" Tito asked.

"You're joking, right?" Kennin smiled as he pulled his new racing gear out of his locker and stuffed it into a black nylon duffel bag.

"I'm just checking," Tito said. "I mean, it's pretty rare to see you get excited about anything."

Outside, Kennin waited while Tito got his bike, then together they started to walk down the sidewalk. Carrying the heavy duffel, there was no way Kennin could ride on Tito's pegs today. A familiar-looking red Lexus IS300 pulled alongside them. The window went down and Mariel said, "Want a ride?"

"Thanks, but today I think I'll walk," Kennin said.

Mariel licked her glossy lips. "You sure?"

"Yeah," Kennin replied.

"Your loss," she said. "See you at the track." She pulled away from the curb.

"You're probably the only guy in the world who's ever said no to her," Tito said with a groan.

Kennin only wished he'd been able to say no to her more often.

They got to Rivera's Service Center. Kennin walked into the garage and was surprised to find the Corolla on a trailer hitched to Cousin Raoul's beat-up white van. The Corolla's hood was up and Angelita, in coveralls, was still tinkering with the engine while Raoul threw spare tires in the back of the van.

"What's this?" Kennin asked.

"Hey, Kennin!" Raoul grinned widely, revealing his crooked white teeth. "You amped or what?"

"What's with the trailer?" Kennin asked.

"We're not street legal," Angelita explained, wiping some soot from her cheek.

"Where'd it come from?" Kennin asked.

"I got it," Raoul said.

"Where?" Kennin asked.

"A friend," Tito's cousin answered.

Kennin and Angelita shared a look. Tito's sister blinked with astonishment, as if she hadn't realized until now just what that meant.

"I'm sorry, Kennin," she apologized. "I was so busy getting the car ready, it never occurred to me."

"What didn't occur to you?" Tito asked, still not getting it.

"Raoul, seriously," Kennin said. "This 'friend' you got the trailer from . . . was it the same friend who gave you the GTO and the Camry?"

Raoul screwed up his face as if trying to come up with an answer.

Now even Tito understood. "Raoul, what did you think you were doing?"

"I was just trying to help," his cousin answered.

"Can we get the car there without the trailer?" Kennin asked.

Angelita shook her head. "No tags, no registration, no insurance, and very little exhaust system."

"Guess we're stuck with the trailer," Kennin said, and turned to Raoul. "When we get to the track, be sure to park this thing way off in the corner of the paddock where it won't be noticed."

They finished tossing the tires and other gear into the van. Angelita was still under the hood.

"It's time to go, Angie," Tito said impatiently.

"Soon," his sister answered.

Tito turned to Kennin and gestured to his watch.

"Every mother has to let her baby go sooner or later," Kennin kidded.

"Okay, okay." Angelita backed away from the car and lowered the hood.

Kennin and Tito got into the back of the van and sat on milk crates amid the tires and other gear. Angelita got into the front with Raoul.

"I can't frickin' believe this!" Tito said excitedly as they headed toward the strip. "I mean, tonight we're gonna do an actual tandem event with sponsors and everything! Think about how far we've come, dude."

Kennin smiled weakly. They might have come farther faster if Tito hadn't sabotaged his own sister's car, but there was no point in reminding Tito of that. Anyway, it hardly mattered now. Tonight was the end.

Ticket booths had been set up at the entrance to the Babylon's new track, and already the line of cars was three and four deep.

"Can you frickin' believe this?" Tito gasped.

Signs proclaimed that the entrance fee for tonight's event was fifteen dollars. Raoul waited in line and then drove up to one of the booths. The ticket taker inside craned his neck out to look at the trailered Corolla. "Competitor?"

Raoul nodded.

"You should have a competitor's pass," the ticket taker said.

"I've got it." Kennin dug into the duffel bag and came up with the bright yellow pass.

"Okay," said the ticket taker. "Drive in and make a right."

Signs directed the fans to the left and competitors to

the right. In the fan parking area, people were having tail-gate parties. Smoke rose from hibachis, and the scent of grilled meat was in the air.

"I just can't frickin' believe this," Tito said as Raoul steered the van and trailer into the paddock, where two dozen cars were parked and crews were busy jacking up rear ends and changing tires. "It's, like, real! A real frickin' drift event!"

"I wish I had a dollar for every time you said the word 'frickin','" Angelita joked.

"Look at that!" Tito pointed at a candy apple red con-vertible. "A frickin' Viper! You see that? Someone's drifting a Viper! And there's a GTO and a Mustang. You believe that crap? And there's an SC300! And a 300 Z! I'm dying! I swear! But it's okay! I can go to heaven now!"

"Cool points, Tito," Kennin reminded him.

"Yeah, sure, right," Tito said, calming for an instant before growing amped again. "Hey, look, there's Chris with *Slide or Die.*"

Chris was wearing a red and black racing suit. His car, as always, sparkled. But it wasn't the same as the last time Kennin had seen it. Like his racing jacket, Chris's car was covered with stickers from Cooper Tires, ACT clutches, Western Automotive, CIT Racing, and others. The largest sticker of all was the scripted "Babylon Drift Team."

They parked, and Angelita climbed into the Corolla to back it off the trailer. Darkness was falling and the track lights went on. The crowd began to file into the seats and a loudspeaker over the paddock announced that practice runs were beginning.

"Ready?" Angelita asked.

Wearing his blue and white Nomex driving suit, Kennin circled the car, inspecting it. In particular, he wanted to make sure the lug nuts were tight. Already the air was filled with the screeching of tires and the revving of engines as cars began their practice laps. Feeling the tug of speed, Kennin got into the car and clipped himself into the harness. The Corolla started on the first turn of the key and revved sweetly. Angelita had tuned the twin-charged engine to peppy perfection. He let the clutch out, and the little beast practically leaped. It might not have had the power of a Viper, but it would be nimbler and quicker than almost every other car there.

But the car's lightness and power had unexpected side effects. On the track, Kennin immediately began to have problems, almost spinning into the wall and losing control and sailing sideways into the midfield, sending dozens of orange cones flying. Chris had been right the day he'd first tried the course. The turns were set up so that you could barely get into second gear. If anything, the course was set up even tighter than it had been the day Kennin had first watched Chris drive it. The emphasis was on corners, not speed, and the Corolla was inclined to oversteer.

But it wasn't just the car or the course. This was the

first time he'd driven like this since the crash, and his nerves were raw. Each time he pushed the Corolla close to the edge of control, his thoughts were plagued with memories of the crash and the excruciating pain that had followed. For the first time in his life Kennin felt tight and uncertain. That light, deft touch he usually felt was gone.

At the end of his practice runs, Kennin found concerned faces waiting for him in the paddock.

"What's wrong?" Tito asked.

"Nothing," said Kennin, still harnessed into the Corolla. "I'm just not used to the handling yet."

"Dude, they're gonna start the individual drift eliminations in a couple of minutes," Tito said. "You *gotta* get used to the handling."

"Gee, thanks for telling me," Kennin snapped irritably.

"Is it the suspension?" Angelita asked.

"No, the suspension's fine," Kennin assured her. "She's running great, really."

"Maybe I could camber out the wheels a little more," Angelita said.

"It's not the car," Kennin grunted harshly.

His angry tone caught Angelita by surprise. That was so unlike him.

"Everything okay?" The voice came from the passenger-side window. Kennin turned and found Mariel leaning in.

"Everything's fine," Kennin replied.

"I'm worried about you," Mariel said, as if Angelita

wasn't even there. Kennin turned and looked into Angelita's eyes. They were filled with consternation. Meanwhile, Mariel reached into the car and stroked his arm. "Is there anything I can do?"

"I'll be okay, thanks," Kennin replied.

Angelita backed away from the driver's-side window. Kennin wished there was something he could say. Then he felt Mariel tap him on the shoulder.

"Seriously, is something wrong?" she asked.

"Can I talk to you later?" Kennin asked.

"Sure, honey, whatever you want."

Kennin released the harness and got out of the Corolla. Angelita was sitting in the dark on some tires, with her back to him.

"Hey," he said, sitting down beside her.

Angelita was silent. She wouldn't even look at him.

"Come on," he said. "Talk to me."

"It's not my fault," she said.

"I know." Kennin hung his head. "I'm just . . . I don't know. I haven't driven in a while. I keep thinking about the crash. I don't like the track layout. The whole thing feels wrong."

She still wouldn't look at him. Her head was turned and she was gazing through the dark at Mariel.

"You listening?" he asked.

"I thought you said there was nothing going on between you two," Angelita said without looking at him.

"There isn't," said Kennin.

"It sure looks like there is," Angelita said.

"Don't be deceived," Kennin said.

Angelita gave him a sharp look. "You're just using her, right? I mean, for rides until the bus strike is over."

"I'm not using her," Kennin said. "She offered."

"And you're not using me, either, right?" Angelita asked. "To build you cars and help you drift?"

Kennin slowly shook his head.

"You better not be," Angelita said.

Kennin sensed someone near them and turned to find Derek carrying a half-eaten hot dog in a white paper napkin.

"Hope I'm not interrupting," Derek said, his cheek bulging.

"What can I do for you?" Kennin asked, and stood up.

"Let's take a walk." Derek jerked his head. They walked around to the far side of the Corolla and stood looking at a couple of guys with flashlights working on an El Camino.

"How's it going?" Derek asked.

"You saw how it's going," Kennin replied.

"You think there's a problem with the track layout?" Derek asked. "Something we could adjust?"

"For me or for everyone?" Kennin asked.

Derek narrowed his eyes. "I'm underwhelmed by your lack of appreciation, kid. Mr. Mercado let you keep your job after you messed with his Ferrari, he kept your sorry butt out of jail after that crash, and he gave you five thousand dollars to build your car. If I were you, I might try to change your attitude to gratitude."

"You make it sound like I'm a charity case and you guys have nothing to gain from how I drive," Kennin said.

Derek took a bite of the hot dog and chewed pensively. "What anyone else gains from this ain't your problem, kid. The point is what you're gaining. I'm getting a little tired of reminding you that you're not the only driver around. Now it's time to shape up and do what you're supposed to do."

"Or what?" Kennin asked. "You'll feed me and my sister to the frickin' wolves?"

"Grow up, kid," Derek growled. "This is the real world."

"Is it?" Kennin said. "Or is it just Las Vegas?"

Tito came over. "Hey, uh, sorry to interrupt, but it's time to get ready for the elimination trials."

Kennin gave Derek a curt nod. He and Tito went back to the Corolla.

"What was that about?" Tito whispered.

Kennin shook his head.

"Next question. What's with my sister?" Tito asked.

"What do you care?" Kennin asked.

"She's my sister," Tito said. "I care."

"Then you should be happy," Kennin said, as he pulled open the door and got into the bucket seat.

"Think you'll qualify?" Tito asked.

Kennin gave him an exasperated look.

"You don't qualify, Derek and Mercado are going to be pissed," Tito reminded him.

"Thanks for the advice," Kennin muttered as he got into the harness. "Don't know what I'd do without it."

"I'm just trying to help," Tito said.

"You want to help? Don't loosen anyone's lug nuts," Kennin said, then started up and headed for the track.

It was dark now, and the track lights were high and bright. Mike Mercado had invested a lot of money in DriftVegas. Kennin started his run. The judges were allowing hot starts in the single drift elimination rounds, and he launched the Corolla across the starting line and immediately broke traction. The Corolla was so high-strung that there was no room for error.

The car whipped violently and Kennin fought the wheel, heeling, toeing, and shifting. His ears were filled with the scream of the tires and the whine of the turbo. Halfway through the course he realized why he was driving so hard. He was pissed. At Tito, at Mariel, at Jack the jackass, at Derek, and everyone else who either wanted to use him or get a piece of him. It was never gonna change. As long as he was here, they were gonna find a way to get their fangs into him.

The run ended, and Kennin drove the car back to the paddock. This time Tito had a smile on his face. "You did good, *amigo.*" He reached in and patted Kennin on the helmet.

Kennin got out of the car and pulled off his helmet. Angelita stood a dozen feet away and came no closer. Her lips were pursed into a small flat line. "Looked good that time," she said.

Kennin crouched down and checked the tire treads. Tito clearly had no idea what was going on. Kennin wondered if Angelita did.

Seven drivers were judged good enough to enter the tandem event, which meant that one driver would be given a bye into the second round. Kennin wasn't surprised when that bye went to him. He crossed his arms and leaned against the Corolla, gazing at the stands filled with fans. Tito came toward him, but stopped a dozen feet away.

"You still pissed off?" he asked.

"What can I do for you, Tito?" Kennin asked.

"You should be happy," Tito said. "You made the cut."

"Right," Kennin replied, knowing they would have made sure he made it even if he'd been on a tricycle.

"You gonna watch the other guys run?"

Kennin shook his head. "I'd rather stay here with the car."

Tito frowned and moved closer. "Hey, you don't have anything to worry about," he whispered. "No one's said a word to me. And if they did, I'd tell 'em to go to hell anyway."

Kennin nodded, but it wasn't Tito he was worried about.

"Anyway, looks like you've pretty much killed those tires," Tito said. "I better get a new set on."

Kennin took the opportunity to get a drink, then sat down on the ground with his back against the pile of tires. A dozen yards away Angelita sat on a cooler talking on her cell phone. Tito was taking the tires off the car with the impact wrench when Raoul strolled up out of the dark.

"Where've you been?" Tito asked his cousin.

"Took a walk through the casino," Raoul said. "You know the sports book where they bet on all the games and stuff? Want to know what they're betting on right now? This."

Kennin looked up. "Right now? In the casino?"

"Yeah." Raoul pointed at the people in the stands. "See all these people? Well, there's another whole crowd in the casino watching on a big screen. Only they're laying bets on every heat. It's big money."

"The house giving odds?" Kennin quickly asked.

"Yeah," said Raoul. "They got that Chris guy goin' off at like two to one. Couple of others are in the five-to-one or ten-to-one range."

"What about Kennin?" Tito asked.

"Thirty to one."

"Are they nuts?" Tito asked.

"No one's ever seen drifting before," Raoul said. "They don't know one car from the next or one driver from another. They hear someone talking about who the hot drivers and fastest cars are and they just go bet."

"But thirty to one?" Tito said.

"Almost every other one of these beaters is running four hundred plus horses, while the Corolla's running at nearly half that," Angelita said, joining the discussion. "Meanwhile the smart money's betting on Kennin. If he wins, whoever bet on him is going to get thirty times their money."

"You put up ten bucks, you get back three hundred," Tito said. "Bet a hundred, you win three thousand."

"That's chump change, man," Raoul said. "Guys put up ten grand to get three hundred grand. And the smart money don't do it unless it's close to a sure thing."

"How's it gonna be a sure thing?" Tito asked. "It's a competition. Anything can happen."

"For three hundred thousand, some people will make sure it's a sure thing," Kennin said ominously.

"So you think they're setting you up to win?" Tito asked Kennin.

"Looks that way to me," Kennin said. If they couldn't count on him to tank a competition, then why not count on him to win? Which was why he couldn't stand this scene.

Angelita came toward him. In a low voice, she said, "I know what you're thinking. But what's the point?"

"The point is not to feel like you're someone's frickin' puppet," Kennin answered.

"Too late for that," Angelita said.

"Maybe not," Kennin replied.

It was time for the second round of heats. There were four cars left, and it was no surprise when Kennin pulled the Corolla up to the starting line and found Ian in the white Cressida waiting for him.

"Surprise, surprise," Ian said.

Kennin didn't reply. The easiest way for the sure money to make certain Kennin won was to put him up against the worst driver in the field. Just before this heat was announced, word had come through the paddock that the guy in the white Cressida had won his last heat because the drifter he'd been matched against had buried his front end in the retaining wall. Kennin didn't want to think about whether that was part of the plan too. But it wouldn't have surprised him.

"Ready to eat my smoke, Chinaboy?" Ian taunted him.

"We'll see," Kennin said calmly.

"No ravine walls here to play chicken with," Ian said.

Sitting in the Corolla, Kennin pulled his racing gloves tight.

Ian opened his mouth to say something more, but Kennin revved the Corolla's engine and drowned him out.

"Hey." Derek leaned into the driver's-side window. "Looks like you're starting to get the feel of it."

Kennin nodded back silently. Derek leaned closer and dropped his voice. "I hear the last time you raced this kid, you didn't put in much effort."

"Didn't need to," Kennin replied.

Derek jerked his head at the crowd in the stands. "This time it's not about winning. It's not just about impressing the judges, either. It's about putting on a show."

Kennin gripped the steering wheel tighter.

"Mr. Mercado don't want to be disappointed," Derek said and turned away.

The starter gave the sign.

Tires spinning white smoke, they were off.

In no time, the Cressida was four car lengths ahead. It was pure horsepower, nothing else, and Kennin wasn't particularly worried. The first corner was a wide sweeping right before the course narrowed and the turns grew tighter. Ian started to get the Cressida sideways. Kennin knew instantly that the guy had been practicing. This was a much smoother start to a drift than the last time they'd faced each other.

As Ian slid the Cressida high and wide, Kennin went in tight, starting his drift later, sliding up beside the Cressida at the apex of the turn. Here was the show Derek wanted. This was what the crowds and judges loved—seeing the cars slide side by side. Kennin held the drift until the last possible second and then backed off half a length just as Ian whipped the rear end of the Cressida around. Had Kennin been a foot closer, the Cressida's rear bumper would have smashed into the Corolla's front end.

The Ian of old would have lost it right there, over-steering into a donut. But today Ian swung back just enough for a feint drift to set up for the next turn. Once again, Kennin angled down into the curve, doing a quick feint himself before drifting inside the Cressida. Wheels screamed in clouds of smoke as both cars slid through the turn.

If Ian was going to do what Kennin expected, now was the time. He watched Ian's hands. When Ian let go of the wheel and reached for the shifter, Kennin grabbed the e-brake and whipped the Corolla around. This time there was no doubt in Kennin's mind that Ian had been trying to knock out the Corolla's front end.

They drifted to the left in another tight corner. Kennin was again inside. Ian had definitely improved his drifting technique, but he clearly wanted to stay on the outside of each tandem turn. Kennin expected him to go into another early drift feint.

But just when they were coming out of the drift . . . where Ian should have straightened out and gone into the next feint, the guy cut sharply in to the left, right in front of Kennin.

Kennin couldn't believe what he was seeing. The Cressida was sideways twenty feet in front of him and the Corolla was going close to fifty miles an hour! He was going to T-bone him!

Kennin wrenched the e-brake and swung the Corolla's wheel to the right as hard as he could, and for one crazy instant the cars once again drifted sideways, only each was facing in a different direction.

Kennin wrenched the wheel back around. At the same instant Ian shot into the midfield, smashing through orange cones and sending them flying. The g-forces whipped the Corolla around and sent it sliding sideways. Kennin wasn't sure why he was still on the track, but he powered the Corolla to avoid traction and finished the run with a nice solo drift.

The entire crowd was on its feet, cheering. Kennin could hear them through the open window. His heart was pounding, and sweat seeped out from the head sock and helmet. He had to clench the wheel hard to keep from trembling. Whatever the fans were cheering about had been accidental, plain and simple.

But why complain? Kennin took a deep breath and started to relax. He didn't know whether Ian's attempt to knock him out of the comp had been his own idea or part of someone's larger plan. Right now it didn't matter. He coasted the Corolla back into the paddock. Drivers and crew on both sides stood clapping and banging on the Corolla's roof. People reached in and patted him on the helmet. The words "awesome," "amazing," and "unreal" buzzed around him like flies.

Kennin rolled to a stop. Tito yanked open the Corolla's

door. "That was amazing! Just frickin' amazing!" he gasped. "How did you do that?"

Driftdog Dave was there and patted him on the shoulder. "Dude, I sure hope someone got that on camera, because people are gonna be downloading that off the Internet for years to come."

Even Chris Craven came over and shook his hand. "Nice move. Never seen anything like it."

It was time for the next heat, and things began to look normal again—guys bent into open hoods, changing tires, or just hanging around smoking and talking. But the moment Kennin got out of the Corolla, he sensed something was wrong. Angelita stood stiffly by the spare tires with a hard expression on her face. Kennin scowled at her. Angelita's eyes darted to her right.

Kennin turned to see Detective Neilson step out of the shadows with two uniformed police officers. He swiveled his head around and saw a police cruiser parked a dozen yards away. Raoul was sitting in the backseat with his hands cuffed behind him. Next to the police car was a Las Vegas PD tow truck.

Neilson had a grim expression on his face. "Four thousand dollars, Kennin."

Kennin felt a shiver. Angelita stared at the ground and bit her lip. She looked like she was going to cry. Kennin glanced at Raoul again. In the back of the police cruiser, Tito's cousin hung his head. Neilson must've gotten him on the stolen trailer.

"Don't worry about him," the detective said. "Just tell me how you came up with that kind of money."

Kennin didn't answer. He could hear tires screaming and engines roaring as the next tandem heat went off.

"I asked you a question," Neilson said.

"Am I under arrest?" Kennin asked.

"Where'd the money come from, Kennin?" Neilson asked.

"I don't have to tell you," Kennin replied.

"You'd be doing yourself a big favor if you did," Neilson said.

"How's that?" Kennin asked.

Neilson didn't answer. Instead, he glanced at Angelita. "Think you could give us a moment?"

Angelita nodded and walked toward the track to watch the heat. Neilson stepped closer to Kennin and lowered his voice. With the roar of the cars in the background, Kennin could hardly hear him. "You want her to get busted for receiving stolen property?"

"I don't know what you're talking about," Kennin said.

"How about I bust her for receiving the proceeds from the sale of stolen property?" the detective asked.

"Still don't know what you're talking about," Kennin said.

"How about I tell her where you've been living for the past few weeks?" asked Neilson.

"What's that got to do with anything?" Kennin asked.

"I need some information," Neilson said. "I got you tangentially involved in two stolen cars and four grand in unexplained cash. Maybe you can close your eyes and pretend it didn't happen, but I can't. Now either you start spilling or I turn the screws tighter, understand?"

"And the information I give you helps put Raoul back in the slammer for a dozen years?" Kennin guessed.

Now it was Neilson's turn not to answer.

"The money's got nothing to do with him," Kennin said.

"Where'd it come from?" Neilson asked.

"Someone who wanted to see me drive on this course," Kennin said.

"Why?"

"Because they seem to think that if I'm not here, it won't be as exciting as if I am," Kennin said.

Neilson nodded. "That may be, Kennin, but you still gotta give me something. It's your choice. The GTO, the Camry, or the four thousand bucks."

Kennin stared down at the ground and didn't answer. He wasn't going to give Neilson what he wanted.

"You're making a mistake," the detective warned.

"Not the first time," Kennin said.

Neilson's face tightened like a fist. "This is your last chance. Give me something or I'll impound this car under the terms of the Nevada Contraband Seizure Law."

Kennin looked up, shocked. "On what grounds?"

"Probable cause that it has been used in the commission of a crime," Neilson said. "In this case, the use of ill-gotten drug money or profits from the sale of stolen vehicles."

"You've got no proof," Kennin argued.

"That's the beauty of it, Kennin," Neilson said. "I don't need proof, just probable cause. It's not a criminal violation. It's civil law. You can even get the car back. All you have to do is cough up fifteen hundred bucks."

"I'm supposed to run in another heat in a few minutes," Kennin said.

Neilson slowly shook his head. "Not happening. If you feel you've been unjustly accused, you can request an appeal. Just keep in mind that the burden's on you to prove you weren't involved in any wrongdoing." The detective hesitated. "That is, unless you suddenly remember some names."

Kennin shook his head.

"You're digging yourself in deeper and deeper," Neilson warned.

"Like I have a choice," Kennin replied bitterly.

Neilson straightened up alertly. "You do, Kennin. You can tell me what's really going on."

There was no answer Kennin could give. Neilson pursed his lips and shook his head sadly. "I've told you this before, Kennin. You seem like a good kid who's in a bad spot. I'd like to help you, but only if you help me."

Kennin hung his head. Neilson said something to the two uniformed officers. Then he headed for Angelita. Kennin watched while Neilson spoke to her. He couldn't hear what the detective was saying, but he could see Angelita's face fall as he gave her the news that the Corolla was being impounded. And then Neilson gave her one more piece of information. Angelita's eyes widened and her mouth fell open. She stared in horror at Kennin. Then tears burst out of her eyes and she bolted from the paddock area.

Tito had gone to watch the next heat. He got back to the paddock area just in time to see his sister run away crying and the cops take the keys to the Corolla from Kennin. "What's going on?" he asked Kennin.

Kennin pointed at the police cruiser with Tito's cousin in the back. "They got Raoul and they're impounding the car."

"What?" Tito gasped. "They can't do that!"

Other drifters and crew started to gather as the word spread that the Corolla was being impounded by the cops. Meanwhile, two guys had gotten out of the police department tow truck and were winching the Corolla.

"It's DQ time," Ian said with a satisfied smile.

"That is so unfair," said Driftdog Dave. "Dude, you can use my car. I probably wouldn't even have it if it wasn't for you."

Kennin shook his head. "You're still in this competition. You should drive."

Seemingly out of nowhere, Derek lumbered up to Neilson and began speaking in hushed, excited tones. Neilson listened, then shook his head. Derek grew more agitated, gesturing and stamping his foot on the ground. It was obvious that he had a lot to lose if the Corolla went away. But no matter what he said, Neilson wasn't to be swayed. Finally the detective turned and walked away.

Mariel came through the crowd. Kennin watched how her eyes went to Chris first before she turned to him. "I hear you need a car?" She reached into her bag and handed him a set of keys on a black Lexus fob. "Here you go."

For a split second Kennin was tempted. A production IS300 might stand a chance. He stared at the keys in his palm and then at Chris, who had an annoyed look on his face, as if he knew she was doing this just to annoy him. That's all it would ever be with her. Kennin should have known that all along. He handed Chris the keys.

"This is your problem," he said, and then turned to go.

"Where're you going?" Tito asked, hurrying behind him.

"To find your sister," Kennin answered.

"What about the competition?"

"I just lost my car, remember?" Kennin said, walking through the paddock, looking for Angelita.

"What about Mariel's Lexus?" Tito said.

"No way," Kennin said. "I've had enough of that BS to last a lifetime."

"Then why are you looking for my sister?" Tito asked.

Kennin didn't answer.

"You promised you'd leave her alone," Tito said.

"That's when I thought you really cared about her," Kennin said.

"You saying I don't care about her?" Tito sputtered.

"If you did, you'd want her to be happy," Kennin said. "And you wouldn't be so quick to sabotage her car."

"I told you, I was forced to do that," Tito said.

"I don't think you argued too hard," Kennin said.

"But . . ."

Kennin didn't listen. It didn't matter what Tito said now. The police tow truck started up and pulled the Corolla out of the paddock. Kennin found Angelita sitting against a fence in the dark behind the stands.

"Can't see much from here," he said.

"Go away," she said.

"I lied to you because I didn't want to hurt you," he said.

"Gee, thanks," she shot back bitterly.

"I'm finished with all that now," he said.

"Oh, sure," Angelita said. "I believe every word."

Engines were revving in the background. Another heat was about to go off.

"I want to go with you," Kennin said.

Angelita looked up in the dark with a puzzled expression on her face. "Where?"

"Wherever you go," Kennin said.

"Why?" she asked.

"You know why," Kennin said.

Angelita stared at him. "How do I know you're telling the truth?"

"What reason would I have to lie?" Kennin asked.

"Excuse me," a voice said in the dark.

Kennin turned to find a man in a gray uniform. It was Joe, one of the security guards from the Babylon. "Kennin Burnett?"

"Yes?" Kennin said.

"Mr. Mercado wants to see you," the guard said.

Kennin looked at Angelita.

"It's okay," she said. "You can go."

Kennin turned back to the guard. "She comes too."

"Mr. Mercado said just you," the guard said.

"I don't go if she doesn't go," Kennin said.

Joe led them through a service entrance at the back of the casino and up in an elevator the room service waiters used. The outer office of the penthouse was dark and Laney's desk was empty. Joe knocked on the wooden door and Mike Mercado answered it. His sleeves were rolled back and his tie was askew, and he looked like he'd had a long day.

"Who's this?" he asked, glancing at Tito's sister after Joe left.

"This is my friend Angelita," Kennin said. "I wanted you to meet her. She's the one who built the car I was driving."

Mercado extended his hand. "Hello, Angelita. I see Kennin has good taste."

Angelita blushed, and Mercado asked them to come in and sit down. Kennin noticed that the curtains were pulled back. From his office at the top of the casino, you could see the lights of Las Vegas and the silhouettes of the mountain peaks in the distance.

"So, Kennin," he said once they'd settled down. "I assume you have something to tell me?"

"I'm leaving town," Kennin said.

Mercado nodded.

"And I didn't use the entire five grand on the car," Kennin said.

Mercado smiled. "Didn't expect you to."

Kennin blinked. "Serious?"

"This is Las Vegas, Kennin," Mercado said. "Everyone cons everyone. The only way you survive is by staying one con ahead. But I appreciate your honesty. So what did you do with the rest of the money?"

"I paid someone I trust to take my sister to LA and put her in a drug rehab," Kennin said. "I'll pay you back."

Mercado grinned. "You already have."

Kennin frowned.

"We did twice what we expected at the gate tonight," Mercado said. "Maybe as much as forty thousand."

"You're not mad?" Kennin asked.

"Mad? I'm delighted!" Mercado said. "Why would you think I'd be mad?"

"The odds were against me," Kennin said. "Everyone expected me to lose. Whoever's betting for me lost a lot of money when I dropped out."

Mercado raised an eyebrow. "Who said you were dropping out?"

"The cops took the car."

Mercado smiled and stood up. "Come over here." He walked to the windows and pointed down. Kennin and Angelita saw the lighted drift track below. The police tow truck had returned to the paddock and the guys in the coveralls were lowering the Corolla.

"How?" Kennin began to ask.

Mercado smiled and patted him on the shoulder. "This is Las Vegas, Kennin."

They turned away from the window. "There's just one thing," Kennin said. "I hope you don't expect me to outdrift Chris Craven's 240 SX."

"If that's what happens, so be it," Mercado said.

"But the betting . . . ," Kennin said.

"The house wins either way," the casino owner said. "We get a percentage of every wager. Win or lose, we make money."

Mercado led Kennin and Angelita toward the doors. "I was impressed with your driving against that idiot in the Cressida. What was his problem? Looked like he was more interested in smashing into you than he was in winning."

"It's a long story, sir," Kennin said.

Mercado opened the door for them. "Sure I can't talk you into hanging around?"

"Thanks, Mr. Mercado," Kennin replied, sliding his arm around Angelita's waist. "But it's time for us to get going."

"California, huh?" Mercado said.

Kennin was surprised, until he realized that he'd said he sent Shinchou there. "We have to establish residence so Angelita can go to college."

"And what about you?" the casino owner asked.

"I don't know," Kennin said with a shrug. "Guess I'll do something with cars."

"You need a reference, I'll be glad to give you one," Mercado said.

"Thanks," Kennin said. "Really. Thanks for everything."

"My pleasure," Mercado said. "Just one thing. Give me a call or drop me a line once in a while, okay? Just to let me know you're okay."

"Sure thing."

Mercado patted Kennin on the shoulder again. "Now go down and run the last heat."

Tito was waiting for them when they got back to the paddock.

"What's going on?" he asked, looking back and forth from Angelita to Kennin.

"Nothing you need to know about right now," his sister said, as she glanced over at the Corolla.

"First the cops take the car away, then they bring it back," Tito said, bewildered.

"Strange how that happens, huh?" Kennin said, picking up his helmet.

Over the loudspeaker they were announcing the final heat.

"Guess I better get going," Kennin said, and got into the Corolla.

Angelita reached into the car and patted him on the helmet. "Have fun."

He lined up next to Chris in *Slide or Die*. The two drivers nodded at each other.

Derek stepped between the cars and bent down so he could speak to both drivers at the same time. "Glad you two could make it," he said, obviously pleased that Kennin and Chris were running against each other in the final heat. "Now remember. It's not just about winning. It's about the show."

Suddenly Derek must have heard something that made him straighten up. "What the hell?" he grumbled. Kennin looked in the rearview mirror and saw Detective Neilson and a uniformed police officer coming toward them. From the look on Neilson's face, Kennin could tell it wasn't good news.

Derek quickly spun to the starter and gave him a nod. Then he rushed toward the detective, blocking his path.

The starter raised his hand and quickly dropped it.

The heat was on.

Putting on a show meant popping the clutch and spinning the tires to create the squeals the crowd loved to hear and the smoke they wanted to see. But drifting against Chris meant that Kennin had to make a decision. Generally, Kennin preferred to be the chaser, staying behind the other car and pressing the lead driver harder and harder to perform until the driver lost either his control of the vehicle or his nerve.

But up against Chris in a 240 SX beater running nearly five hundred horsepower, it would be hard to apply much pressure. It was more likely that Chris would jump out to a lead and put on a major drifting show while Kennin struggled to keep up. The only choice Kennin had was to go into the lead and see what happened.

But even that wasn't going to be easy. With all that horsepower, Chris was quickly five car lengths ahead when he started drifting into the first turn. Kennin should have drifted too, but with five car lengths between them, it wasn't exactly tandem. Given all Mike Mercado had done for him, the least Kennin could do was put on a show.

While Chris drifted sideways through the first corner, Kennin shot low past him on the inside, coming out with a late drift in the straightaway while Chris whipped around and chased him.

Kennin had no doubt that Chris wasn't happy to see him blitz that turn. To the untrained eye it probably looked like Kennin, in the smaller, slower car, was showing him up. Chris took the bait and charged after him, tucking the 240 SX in tight as they plowed through the next turn. With barely inches between the Corolla's rear bumper and Chris's front end, they whipped around the next corner, Kennin bracing himself and turning the wheel hard while heel-and-toeing to keep the rpms over four thousand.

Out of the corner of his eye he saw Neilson and a uniformed cop standing at trackside, watching. Something about the way the detective's arms were crossed and the steely gaze in his eyes confirmed what Kennin had already suspected—they were waiting for him. And this time Kennin wasn't going to be able to talk his way out of it.

But that would be later. Right now, an unrelenting Chris Craven bore down on him, pushing harder and harder through each turn, forcing Kennin into more and more extreme drifts. As they went into the next corner, Kennin forced the front end of the Corolla deep into the curve. He could feel the rear end swing out, and the tires screamed, giving off a cloud of smoke so thick he could no longer see the car chasing him.

Suddenly the rear end slipped. In an instant Kennin knew he'd burned through the tire tread to the steel belt below. The Corolla started to spin. The engine stalled, and in no time Kennin was backward in a thick cloud of smoke. A split second later the bright red nose of _Slide or Die_ came through the haze straight at him.

Crunck! Chris's front bumper smashed into Kennin's, punching the Corolla backward, the impact driving Kennin's face into the steering wheel.

Both cars stopped on the track, facing each other. Kennin felt a bolt of pain across the bridge of his nose and warm moisture began to course over his lips. He had a feeling his nose was broken, but right now the pain wasn't too bad. Meanwhile, the crowd in the stands had gone silent. The only sounds were _Slide or Die_'s idling engine and the clink and clatter of broken pieces of car body falling to the ground.

As the last of the smoke drifted away, Kennin stared through the windshield at Chris. They locked eyes, and suddenly Kennin had a feeling they were thinking the same thing. It was all about the show. And if the cars would still run, why not give it to them?

Kennin twisted the key in the ignition and restarted the

Corolla. He jammed it into reverse, punched the accelerator, and whipped the nose around. Centrifugal forces sent more pieces of car skittering over the asphalt. Was it his imagination, or did he actually hear the crowd roar with delight? With the dented nose of the 240 SX tight on his tail, he gunned the Corolla into the next turn, the right front fender clanging and flapping like a bird with a broken wing.

This time Chris came around the outside, the front bumper of *Slide or Die* hanging at an angle like a crooked smile. They both careened through the next turn, the torque and g-forces causing the broken cars to groan and wobble. Something long and red flew past Kennin. It had to be Chris's bumper.

Both cars powered out of the turn side by side while a couple of pit crew guys jumped onto the asphalt to clear away the debris. The next corner was a hairpin right. In unplanned synchronicity Kennin and Chris both feinted left and yanked hard on their wheels. *Thwank!* The momentum of the heavier 240 SX slammed it sideways into the Corolla. Kennin was jarred, but he somehow managed to keep control. He hated to think of what the left side of *Slide or Die* looked like. One thing was certain: Chris's car was no longer a glossy, lacquered thing of beauty.

Out of the hairpin they swept together into a left, doors nearly touching. Running on the steel belts, the Corolla made sounds Kennin had never heard before, throwing showers of hot orange sparks. As they came out of the turn,

Kennin knew the tires were in their death throes. Both cars were right in front of the stands. There was only one thing left to do.

He gunned the Corolla's engine, veered off to the right, and then, in a pyrotechnic shower of sparks and smoke, snapped the car back into a 180. *Pow! Pow!* One after another the rear tires blew. Meanwhile, Chris took the hint and veered to the left and did the same. Bands of steel and chunks of black rubber flying, the cars screeched together and came to a stop, facing the direction from which they'd come.

The crowd went crazy. Kennin climbed out of the Corolla. What was left of the tires was still smoking, and shreds of steel bands glowed red hot. He pulled off his helmet and the head sock, damp and darkened with blood. Chris got out of *Slide or Die*.

"You okay?" he asked when he saw Kennin.

"Yeah. It's just a little blood."

Chris smiled. "Guess we gave them a show."

"Looks like it," said Kennin, aware that Detective Neilson was approaching with the uniformed officer, who was pulling a pair of black handcuffs off his belt.

"Turn around and put your hands behind your back," Neilson said.

Kennin did as he was told.

"What's going on?" Chris asked.

Neilson ignored him. "Kennin Burnett, I am arresting

you for grand theft auto. You have the right to remain silent. Anything you say can and will be used against you in a court of law. You have the right to speak to an attorney, and to have an attorney present during any questioning. If you cannot afford a lawyer, one will be provided for you at government expense."

Angelita and Tito arrived. "What's this for?" Angelita asked.

"Something I didn't do," Kennin replied.

"Kennin, take my advice," Neilson said. "Remain silent. How's that nose?"

"Not sure."

"We'll have a look at it down at the station."

The police officer slid his hand around Kennin's arm just above the elbow and led him to a cruiser. Kennin glanced over his shoulder at Angelita. "Sorry about the car."

"I wouldn't worry about it now," she said. "What should I do?"

"Wait for me," Kennin said as the cop put him in the back of the cruiser.

26

They took him in the back door at the Las Vegas Metro police station. There was no perp walk through the front doors with photographers taking pictures and reporters shoving microphones in his face. The only photos were the mug shots taken by the police photographer. But first they cleaned the blood off and put a bandage on his nose. The cop who did it said he was pretty sure it was broken.

Afterward, Kennin was fingerprinted and led by the officer into a small room with two chairs, a metal table, a video camera on a tripod, and a large mirror. Welded into the top of the table was a steel ring roughly the diameter of a baseball.

"I can make it a little more comfortable for you," the cop said.

"Thanks," said Kennin.

The cop unlocked the cuffs. "Sit down."

Kennin sat. The cop slid the empty cuff through the steel ring, then recuffed it to Kennin's wrist. He was still handcuffed, but at least now his arms were resting on the table in front of him, instead of behind his back.

The door opened and Detective Neilson came in. He'd taken off his jacket and rolled up his sleeves. The detective turned to the cop. "Video camera loaded?"

"Yes, sir," the cop replied.

"Get it going," Neilson said.

"Yes, sir." The cop aimed the camera at Kennin and pressed a button. A small red light on the recorder went on.

"I assume you've seen enough cop shows to know how this works, Kennin," Neilson said, sitting down at the table across from Kennin. "This is where I interview you about the case."

Kennin glanced at the mirror. Thanks to the crash, his eyes had blackened, and under the white bandage his nose had swollen to double its normal size.

"Yeah, there are a couple of people back there," Neilson said. "But that's more for me than you. They're gonna grade me on my interviewing technique."

"You sure there isn't an assistant DA in there trying to get a handle on the case and decide whether or not there's enough evidence to go ahead?" Kennin asked.

Neilson smiled slightly. "Guess you do watch those TV shows."

"Guess so," Kennin said, not amused.

The detective leaned forward and placed his elbows on the table. "First of all, please tell the camera how your nose got broken. We don't want any police brutality crap."

Kennin explained what had happened on the track.

"Thanks," Neilson said. "Now, I don't want to say I told you so, Kennin, but you and I both know I did. I told you someday we'd get someone who knew something about that GTO or the Camry and then I'd bring you in, didn't I?"

Kennin imagined poor Cousin Raoul, who was undoubtedly facing a parole violation and some serious jail time.

"We went back and dusted the Camry again," Neilson said. "This time we got a print off the rearview mirror. We brought the suspect in and he spilled about how you helped wipe the Camry and unload the GTO."

Kennin wasn't surprised that Raoul gave him up but not Tito. Blood was thicker than water.

"I didn't boost the car," Kennin said.

"At the very least you're an accomplice," the detective said. "Plus, I can make a pretty good case with the GTO on reckless endangerment and resisting arrest. Now, you have a choice. You can refuse to cooperate and take your chances with some court-appointed, government-paid lawyer who probably bought his diploma at the University of Kmart. Or you can play ball. It's up to you."

"And if I play ball, what happens?" Kennin asked.

"Depends on how good your information is," Neilson said.

Kennin gazed down at the table. Everybody knew this

was what the cops did. They worked their way up the food chain, "turning" each successive fish against the next until they got to the big guys. Kennin would never rat out a friend, but on the other hand he wasn't about to take the fall for cars he didn't steal. What did he have to give?

He had Tito, a friend, but also a jerk who'd almost gotten him killed. But Tito was Angelita's brother, and Kennin wouldn't do that to her.

He had a bunch of illegal street drifters, including a bigot named Ian. But if he gave up Ian, there was a good chance Ian would give up guys like Driftdog Dave and Micky Shift 'n' Slide.

"Come on, Kennin, you gotta have something," Detective Neilson urged him.

Kennin shook his head. There was no one he could give up with a clear conscience.

"They won't let you off with youthful offender status here." Neilson increased the pressure. "You're looking at time in juvenile detention. And with you in juvie, who's gonna keep an eye on your sister?"

Kennin remained tight-lipped. Neilson frowned and looked disappointed. He waved to the cop, who was standing in the corner beside the video camera. "Turn it off."

Neilson left the room. Kennin had a feeling he'd gone to speak to whoever was behind the one-way mirror. But he had no way of knowing for certain. A few minutes later the detective returned.

"Should I turn the camera back on, sir?" the cop asked.

"No." Neilson grabbed the chair and slid it around until it was close to Kennin. He sat down so close that their shoulders touched. "Listen carefully, Kennin," he said in a rough whisper. "I don't know if you took that car yourself, or just got stuck getting rid of it. That would be something a jury would decide—if it ever gets to a jury, which it won't, because your lawyer is gonna twist your arm so hard to cop a plea you'll wind up with two left hands. Frankly, you don't seem like a bad kid to me. Mostly I think you've made some bad decisions and had a lot of lousy breaks. The problem is, there's only so much I can do for you. The mayor wants results, and so does the chief of police. Now, I can either go back and say 'I nailed the creep who stole the mayor's wife's car,' or I can go back and say, 'Hey, I found the creep who took the car and leaned on him and he gave up this real badass.' But it's got to be one or the other."

The room became quiet.

Real badass . . . , Kennin thought.

Then he smiled. Why hadn't he thought of Jack the jackass sooner?

27

A little after one a.m. two days later, Detective Neilson drove Kennin, Angelita, and Tito to the Las Vegas bus station on South Main Street. Kennin and Angelita were scheduled to take the one forty-five a.m. bus to San Fernando, California, not far from where Shinchou was in rehab. They carried the luggage, mostly Angelita's, inside.

The bus station was nearly empty. A few travelers waited for late-night buses, and a couple of bums slept on the benches. Kennin and the others stopped near the gate for the bus, which had not yet arrived. Neilson reached into his pocket and handed them each an envelope.

"Here are your tickets," he said. "Sorry you can't stay for graduation, Angelita, but the faster you leave town, the better. We'll make sure they send you your diploma."

"Thanks," said Kennin. His eyes were still blackened,

and he still had the bandage on his nose, but the swelling had started to subside.

"Hey, I should be thanking you," said Neilson. "The testimony you and your sister gave is going to help put Jack and his friends away for a long time. We got it all on tape."

"No chance of him finding out where it came from?" Kennin asked.

"No way," said Neilson. "We've made sure of that. Plus, I'm the only one who'll have your address and phone number in California. Even your families will have to go through me to contact you."

"What about seeing them?" Angelita asked.

"We'll help you arrange that in an undisclosed location," the detective said.

Behind them a bus pulled up to the gate and a loudspeaker announced, "The bus to Barstow, San Bernardino, Pasadena, San Fernando, Glendale, and Los Angeles is now boarding."

"I'll give you guys some privacy," Neilson said, and stepped away.

Tito shoved his hands into his pockets. "Well, I guess this is it."

Angelita gave him a hug. "Don't look so sad. We'll stay in touch."

"Maybe I'll come out there and visit," Tito said.

"Definitely," said Angelita.

"I gotta say something in private to Kennin, okay?" Tito said.

"Sure." Angelita kissed him on the cheek and then climbed onto the bus.

Tito waited until she was out of earshot, then looked up at Kennin. "Look, I know I really screwed up. There's no excuse for what I did, and I just want to say I'm sorry." He held out his hand.

Kennin smiled and shook it.

"Think you'll do some drifting out there?" Tito asked.

"Can't seem to avoid it," Kennin said.

"Then maybe that's the way it's meant to be," Tito said.

"Maybe," Kennin answered. The loudspeaker announced that the bus was ready to leave.

"Take good care of my sister, okay?" Tito asked.

"You bet." Kennin climbed onto the bus. Angelita was sitting about halfway back, next to the window. He sat down beside her.

"What'd he say?" she asked.

"Just that I should take care of you," Kennin answered.

"He's such a kid," Angelita said.

"Yeah."

The bus pulled out of the station and into the Las Vegas night. As it headed out of town, the lights of the strip grew dimmer.

"I can't say I'll miss this place," Angelita said.

"Me neither," said Kennin. And yet, even as the words left his lips, he had the strangest feeling that he'd be back.

Todd Strasser is the author of more than one hundred twenty books for teens and middle graders, including the bestselling Help! I'm Trapped In . . . series, and numerous award-winning YA novels, including *The Wave*, *Give a Boy a Gun*, and *Can't Get There from Here*. As a boy, Todd was a fan of international Formula One grand prix and GT racers such as Graham Hill, Jim Clark, and Jackie Stewart. An avid go-cart driver in his youth, Todd went on to drive a variety of motorcycles and sports cars before marriage and children slowed him down.

Learn more about Todd at www.toddstrasser.com.